The G

The Ghost-seer

An Interesting Tale
from the Memoirs of Count von O**

Friedrich von Schiller

Translated by Andrew Brown

ET REMOTISSIMA PROPE

100 PAGES

100 PAGES
Published by Hesperus Press Limited
4 Rickett Street, London SW6 1RU
www.hesperuspress.com

This version first published in German in 1798
This translation first published by Hesperus Press Limited, 2003

Introduction and English language translation © Andrew Brown, 2003
Foreword © Martin Jarvis, 2003

Designed and typeset by Fraser Muggeridge
Printed in the United Arab Emirates by Oriental Press

ISBN: 1-84391-034-9

CONTENTS

Would it surprise you to learn that *The Ghost-seer*, for me, ranks alongside one of the formative works of my childhood as an oddly obscure masterpiece of world literature? Really? Which other prodigious book can I mean? Schopenhauer's *Die Welt als Wille und Vorstellung*? Kant's *Critique of Pure Reason*? No. Just a handy little tome, *The Boy's Book of Conjuring*.

Whatever else Schiller's prose master-work may be, it's assuredly a catalogue of illusion, an examination of truth and deception, mask and face, a glittering Magic Show. Amazingly, all the dazzling tricks this great writer concocts for us are still performed around the world today, in some form or other.

Friedrich von Schiller, entertainer, previously known to many of us only as a world-shattering dramatist, waves a wand across the years and levitates me back to childhood with his astonishing compendium of flying sorcery. He beguiles – with more versions of hocus-pocus, incantation, legerdemain, vanishings and sleight of hand than Chung Ling Soo had hot noodles.

Like those enigmatic members of the Magic Circle, I mustn't give too much away. It's your choice whether you want a preview of Schiller's ghostly 'effects' now or, like me aged eleven, scramble feverishly through the pages to find out how they're done. Though, even after I had gleaned the secrets of some of the world's most astonishing illusions, I would still goggle afresh when I saw them presented. Robert Harbin sawing a woman in half at Croydon's Grand Theatre. With comedy. He produced a large bloodstained cloth and announced, 'I'm sorry, ladies and gentlemen, we had a bit of trouble with this trick at the matinée.' Not so very different from Schiller's mawkish humour as our heroes confront a so-called apparition by firing up the chimney:

'"Jesus and Mary! I'm wounded," repeated the man in the fireplace. The ball had smashed his right leg.'

But what of the Ghost-seer himself, the impoverished German Prince who embarks on Uncle Freddie's Magical Mystery Tour? Some might say he is merely being taken for a ride. It's clear from the text that Friedrich von Schiller was aware of every form of bewitchery right back to Shakespeare's time. He treats his audience to preternatural versions of Banquo's ghost, Hamlet's father, even a monkish flash of Richard II. There's an opening panorama virtually cloned from *The Merchant of Venice*, plus a baffling mini-casket trick that would have upstaged Portia.

Then, abracadabra, in a flash-forward to the nineteen-fifties, thousands of children including me sit, equally captivated, in front of another magic box: our parents' brand new nine-inch Pye television. We don't know it but we're viewing Schiller's fun and games a century and a half on – genial David Nixon linking silver rings; mysterious David Berglas reading our minds; inscrutable Chan Canasta conducting 'occult experiments'. We're all as keen to believe in the truth of these lies as the innocent Prince himself.

Of course then I'd never heard of the eminent German author. Never mind. Unbeknownst, I was mocking up a kind of Junior Schiller handbook myself in our small front room. Eager for Grandma and Grandpa, Mum, Dad, sister Angela, Auntie Patricia and Uncle Cecil to take their places and marvel at my rendition of Mum's disappearing curtain ring, the multiplying billiard balls (well, one of them did) and (the Prince would have loved this) a magic mirror that, incredibly, reflected the playing-card chosen by Grandpa.

Oh yes, while most of my chums were adventuring vicariously via *Biggles*, *Just William* and *Rockfist Rogan*, I devoured every magic manual I could lay my hands on. All Schiller's stuff was there. Smoke and mirrors, fake seances, hidden assistants, as well as crafty cabinets, hand bells with no hands, and all the jiggery-pokery of eighteenth- and nineteenth-century neo-necromancy. When the Sicilian sorcerer manifests a human figure in a bloody shirt cavorting above the fireplace, please remember I attempted my own humble interpretation circa 1953 – the dancing skeleton.

Was my version as complex as Schiller's? Hardly. But I suppose he might allow me to mention that instead of a 'human shape', the bare bones of my illusion were wondrously suspended from somewhere between the end of the mantelpiece and the door to the cupboard under the stairs. Whether there was fishing wire involved and cunningly concealed hooks, I'd better not say. And if, as in *The Ghost-seer*, the darkened room and flickering firelight were essential to the suspension of disbelief, well, I must leave you to make up your own mind. But whatever *frisson* (or not) Uncle Cecil, Auntie Patricia and all experienced in our suburban lounge as they staggered in after Christmas lunch, they were, in essence, witnessing a mini-variant of Schiller's chicanery.

Or am I trying to mislead you? It's a magician's trick after all, the art of misdirection. Maybe, as box after box in this portmanteau collection is unlocked, a new truth is exposed that distorts the one that went before. Well – no, no, I really mustn't divulge. Except to whisper there are many mysteries within to guess at. Who really is, for example, the Madonna-like young woman encountered by our hero in the chapel? A ghost? He, after all, is the ghost-seer. Isn't he? Also, what is the secret of the young Marchese's disappearance? How significant are the devilish transmutations in the character of the Prince? And why do we fear the strange Armenian?

I'm still saying nothing.

Schiller is a joyous storyteller who, I believe, has passed on his dexterous skills down the years to writers such as Dickens, Wilkie Collins, Bram Stoker, Wilde and Pirandello. These literary magi have all created scenarios where nothing is necessarily as it appears to be; in which an event, a character, an idea may head us towards something alarmingly unexpected.

Some of his images have transcended time. Who, in Wilde's *The Sphinx Without a Secret*, is the seraphic vision of loveliness we glimpse hurrying along Bond Street? Surely none other than a reincarnation of that same irresistible saint who so obsesses the Prince. It is in the quiet church adjoining the Giudecca gardens that suddenly, all artifice aside, the genius of Schiller's writing persuades us it may be possible to find God in other people.

Clearly, like Ebenezer Scrooge (a 'ghost-seer' created some forty years later), we are free to cry, 'No such thing as ghosts. Bah! Humbug!' Until, in this gloriously operatic set of conundrums, we catch ourselves assessing the impassive features of that wandering Armenian. We consider his ageless, timeless existence; the drops of blood on his shirt; his apparent invisibility upon the stroke of midnight. Bah! Hum –

And yet, and yet…

But then, is anything really what it seems, in this ultimate book of conjuration? Just be careful. And watch out for all Friedrich von Schiller's cunning threads – a glistening web of construction, hanging, mid-air, somewhere between the fireplace, the altar and the dark cupboard under the stairs.

– Martin Jarvis, 2003

In 1766 the great German philosopher Immanuel Kant published a short and intriguing work under the title *Träume eines Geistersehers, erläutert durch Träume der Metaphysik*. The standard translation of this title runs: *Dreams of a Spirit-seer, elucidated by Dreams of Metaphysics*, but the word here rendered as 'spirit-seer' is the same one – *Geisterseher* – that I have translated as 'ghost-seer' in the later work by Friedrich von Schiller (final edition: 1798). What are we talking about when we talk about spirits, or ghosts? Kant's essay focuses precisely on this issue, and he addresses the existence both of spirits (in the sense of disembodied centres of consciousness) and of ghosts (in the sense of uncanny apparitions). *Can* we intelligibly talk about either, when their status is so ambiguous (are they mental or physical, dead or alive, subjective or objective, natural or supernatural, illusory or real)? What does it mean to claim that one 'believes in ghosts'? What *rational* objections can be made to their existence? One would be this: the concept of a disembodied entity that can nonetheless be perceived by the senses of an embodied human being is incoherent. And what *empirical* objections? One might run: almost all cases involving the 'supernatural' turn out, on investigation, to be explicable by purely natural causes, and in many cases to be the product of deliberate deception on the part of some impostor.

The particular *Geisterseher* that Kant wished to subject to his powerful philosophical scrutiny was his long-lived near-contemporary, Emanuel Swedenborg (1688–1772). Swedenborg began his productive career as a Swedish scientist, well-versed in the study of nature, mathematics and the technological innovations of the early eighteenth century: a widely travelled, sociable, cosmopolitan figure who in many ways embodied what was to become the ideal of the Enlightenment man of reason and experiment, adept in the abstractions of algebra but equally able to turn his hand to practical inventions. His labyrinthine ingenuity found ample scope when he started to publish Sweden's first real scientific journal, the aptly named *Daedalus Hyperboreus*. For thirty years he was occupied in the administration and improvement of his country's mining industry, but still found time to travel and develop his increasingly complex speculations on the nature of the world, which, published as the *Principia Rerum Naturalium* (*Principles of Nature*) in some ways anticipated modern physics in its vision of matter as composed of infinitely divisible, swirling particles – just as he also proposed ideas about the way the sun, and its orbiting planets, originated in a single nebula (a theory that was further developed by Kant and Laplace), and did research into animal and human physiology and psychology that looked forward to later investigations into the localisation of thought processes in the brain. But however good his credentials as a scientist, Swedenborg's impact – seen in the influence he had on profoundly counter-Enlightenment thinkers such as Blake, Balzac, Baudelaire, Emerson, Yeats and Strindberg – was the result of a religious crisis documented in his *Journal of Dreams* (1743–4), which relates his dreams and visions, his spiritual experiences and his powerful sexual fantasies and obsessions. A vision of Christ in 1744 led to his decision to abandon his scientific interests: thereafter he devoted himself to voluminous tomes subjecting the Bible to his own idio-syncratic but systematic interpretations, and explicating his view of the 'correspondences' between the physical world and the celestial realm: the *Principles of Nature* gave way to – or were supplemented by (as Swedenborg never lost the habit of writing in a dispassionate, curiously analytical way even about angels and spirits) – the *Heavenly Arcana*, the *Apocalypse Explained, On Heaven and its Wonders and On Hell*. By the 1780s there was a Swedenborgian 'church' in London. It still exists.

It was not just as a speculative theologian that Swedenborg attracted the interest of his contemporaries, however, but as a mystic who experienced at first hand the paranormal. Kant was fascinated partly by the theology – what credence could be given to Swedenborg's spirit world? – and partly by the clairvoyance: thus he recounts some of the most celebrated anecdotes concerning Swedenborg's gifts of second sight and precognition. In 1759 Swedenborg had just returned from England to Gothenburg (modern Göteborg) in Sweden, and at a gathering in the house of a merchant the same evening, suddenly became profoundly agitated, announcing that there was a terrible fire raging in Stockholm, a good 250 miles away; he then left the room, only to return, finally reporting that the fire had been checked. It took two days for the news of the fire to reach Gothenburg: the details agreed with Swedenborg's report. In 1761, summoned by a princess to give proof of his supernatural abilities, Swedenborg discovered something known to her that he himself could have learnt from no living human being. And on another occasion, the widow of a Dutch envoy at the Swedish court asked Swedenborg to discover whether her late husband had in fact paid off a goldsmith's bill for which she was being pestered: Swedenborg, apparently after communication with the spirit world, came back to tell her that a receipt would be found in the hidden compartment of a desk that she thought had been completely emptied.

Kant's attitude to these stories, and to Swedenborg's pretensions to have, as it were, insider knowledge of a world transcending the experience of most ordinary mortals, was a mixture of caustic irony and curious respect. His essay was written at a transitional time in the development of his own thinking: he had become sceptical about the rationalist metaphysics of Leibniz and Wolf, but had not yet embarked on his 'critical' philosophy which would attempt to legislate on what could and could not intelligibly be said about the kinds of vision Swedenborg enjoyed, or the validity of the apparently supernatural experiences to which he was prone. For the time being, Kant is content to comment that however much it may seem a 'contemptible business' for a sensible philosopher even to lower himself to examine such superstitious and credulous nonsense as Herr Swedenborg's fantasies, they are not innately any more dubious than the other 'dreams' he scrutinises with an equally satirical eye – those of metaphysics. Why, he asks, should it be more creditable to be taken in by 'the pretence of reason' than by an 'incautious belief in misleading stories'?

This was not to be Kant's last word on such issues, of course, and his critical philosophy (from the *Critique of Pure Reason* – first edition 1781 – onwards) was to move from the ironic and mutually demystifying juxtaposition of 'metaphysical' and 'mystical' dreams to a much more strenuous and probing attempt to allot distinct spheres of validity to different kinds of language and experience (epistemological, ethical, aesthetic, religious). But his discussion of Swedenborg in *Dreams of a Spirit-seer* anticipates Schiller's *Ghost-seer* in theme as well as title. The Prince in Schiller's tale is brought up a Protestant who has indulged in

Pietistic 'enthusiasm' but, in increasing reaction against the puritanical, life-denying and punitive nature of his childhood religion, becomes at first merely lukewarm to his faith and then, on exposure to mysterious experiences that parallel many of those associated with Swedenborg, demonstrates a fascination for the paranormal. The latter is clearly more alluring than the dreary pieties of German Protestantism, but the Prince also goes out of his way – like a good detective – to find the all-too-human interests that motivate the 'impostors' and their tricks (all done, he claims – and the story tends to corroborate his conclusion – with smoke and mirrors). But just as Swedenborg's life story embodies a conversion narrative, Schiller's tale relates how the Prince goes through a whole sequence of such 'conversions': from devout Protestant to, as it were, sceptical enquirer into the paranormal, then passing through a phase of libertinage in the corrupt but enticing atmosphere of Venice, with its masks and its mirror-makers and its elite intellectual club, the Bucentauro, where even cardinals can apparently indulge in licentious freethinking, and where the Prince tries to make up for his own intellectual 'backwardness' (in some ways that of the petty states of the Holy Roman Empire which Schiller knew all too intimately) by catching up with the latest ideas, only to fall prey, given his lack of independence of mind, to the most garbled and superficial aspects of 'enlightened' thought. (The Prince's oscillations between faith and scepticism, love of magic and wariness towards the 'beyond', religious enthusiasm and nihilistic despair, mirror those of another German hero, Faust: both succumb, at least for a while, to a longing for the intoxications of the fleeting moment as a way of deadening the pain of their conviction that we can know nothing *certain* – part of the crisis, again, that Kant's philosophy tried to register and solve.) And although he had been able to resist the temptations of the supernatural, he seems less immune to the charms of beauty, in the shape of the woman he sees in church. The scene in which he falls in love with her – though he himself, like any good lover, rejects the language of love as being inadequate to the singularity of its object – is clearly a replay of the earlier scene of conjuration in the pavilion down the Brenta. Then, an apparent impostor had exploited the paraphernalia of religion (and more particularly of baroque Catholicism, albeit tinged with

Freemasonry: altar, crucifix, incense, apron, Chaldee Bible, skull, careful effects of light and dark) to create an atmosphere conducive to belief in spectral apparitions and communications with the spirit world. He failed, at least in the Prince's case. But if, as is likely, the same network of impostors, with the fascinatingly demonic Armenian at their head, is *also* responsible for stage-managing this encounter with the woman in the church, the techniques are the same: to induce an openness to 'spirits' (or the Spirit) by exposing the victim to a particularly suggestive atmosphere – in this case, what seems to be Palladio's great church of the 'Redentore', embellished with a beautiful and mysterious woman who clasps the crucifix with the same fervour as the Sicilian in the earlier episode. But in this latter case, the 'trick' works, and the Prince experiences a deluded erotico-mystical flight of fancy – or a profound religious experience – and accepts the supernatural (the Christ figure held in the hand of the beautiful woman).

What is the story ultimately about? It remains unfinished, although, when published in instalments in Schiller's journal *Thalia*, *The Ghost-seer* aroused considerable interest, with the public clamouring for more. Yet Schiller grew increasingly tired of it, and found – not untypically, in his case – that he had become more interested in the philosophical questions it raised than in telling a story: a pity, because the strong and clear narrative line, enlivened by the tales-within-tales, the many parallels, echoes and mirrorings, the masks that hide other masks, the impostor caught out by his own imposture – or is he? – and the growing sense of paranoia, all make Schiller's story, as it stands, an outstanding piece of Gothic fiction. (A long and rather rambling 'Philosophical Conversation from *The Ghost-seer*', now usually – as in my translation – omitted from the story, or published as an appendix, dwelt at length on these more abstract issues.) The Armenian (or Russian, or…), that 'Unfathomable' man of a thousand masks, ageless and ubiquitous, who has drawn his wisdom from the Pyramids, seems for all his supernatural powers to have a very earthly agenda – luring the Prince into a crime that will yield him a crown, perhaps? Or perhaps the Armenian is luring him into the bosom of what the Prince's sister scornfully calls, in a mocking allusion to *extra Ecclesiam nulla salus*, 'the Church outside of which there is no salvation': Catholicism.

For Schiller, as for his age, religion and politics were inseparable – some of the piquancy of the story for his first readers would have stemmed from the fact that the Duchy of Württemberg, predominantly Protestant, had a childless Catholic duke, and the question as to whether his Protestant brother (or *his* offspring) might provide the Duchy with a Protestant ruler was vexed by the fact that the latter's family seemed prone to converting to Catholicism: the Jesuits were, as usual, imagined to be behind it all. But religion and epistemology were inseparable too: if faith declines, can we be sure of anything? The Prince is weak, easily led, and far from embodying the ideal of rational autonomy that Kant – and to some extent Schiller – established as a new moral guiding principle. Schiller may well have meant his story to be a horrible example of how easily such a person – too modern for the old certainties of an 'unexamined' faith but too old-fashioned to be able to grasp the full depth of the philosophical issues at stake and come up with a mature, independent and responsible answer to the temptations of self-indulgent freethinking – is lured, when the hocus-pocus of necromancy fails, to fall back on Catholicism. 'In Rome you will find out' is one of the story's unfulfilled promises. But the Prince's love for the mysterious stranger, however much it may be caught up with a wider nexus of religious and political scheming, goes beyond that. Despite its stereotypical language, it powerfully rekindles Neoplatonic and courtly-love ideas of using beauty – sexual beauty – to awaken a sense of the divine. The 'apparition' in the Redentore is not so different from that of Beatrice Portinari in Florence's Santa Maria dei Fiori, revealing to the young Dante what will be, in more than one sense, the love of his life. Repeatedly, Schiller's story shows how something apparently real turns out to be 'just' a picture, copy, or counterfeit; and yet he sets his story in a country, and a city, which contains some of the most powerful images ever made. Why should they not, like human love, be just as effective in granting intimations of 'another dimension' as are the deliverances of 'reason' and the 'eternal laws of nature' to which the Prince initially appeals?

Schiller's story is a ghost story, but also a love story. Veronese's *Marriage Feast at Cana*, whose power the narrator rather grudgingly acknowledges, is a notoriously sumptuous celebration of human nuptials blessed by divine recognition; and it is a sign that the Prince cannot yet synthesise the fragmented forms of love into a whole when he rejects the Florentine artist's insistence that his three paintings – Madonna, Heloise and Venus – must be brought as a job lot. The three women represent, respectively, heavenly, sacred-and-profane (Heloise, lover of Abelard, as well as mystic and nun), and sexual love: by accepting only the Madonna, the Prince loses them all. Schiller's story is also a story about Spirit and its fraught but all the more intimate relations with flesh; it probes the absurdities to which credulous human beings are prone, but also – perhaps against its own intentions – suggests that the ideal of rational autonomy is meaningless unless it also does justice to our inevitable heteronomy (our enthralment to others – to other worlds, in all their spookiness and at times tawdry allure; to other people; to the various 'others' of reason, such as love and beauty; or quite simply to unreasonable artifices: paintings, music – Biondello's flute – and stories); it suggests the ease with which Catholicism falls prey to superstition, corruption and idolatry while suggesting that the Protestant alternative is not only equally authoritarian and credulous, but doesn't on the whole produce anything like such good visual art.

Hegel, for all his rationalism, wrote, not long after *The Ghost-seer*, of the 'cunning of reason', as if reason behaved not like Schiller's Prince of ** in 'detective' mode, availing himself of the straightforward austerities of logical deduction and scientific methodology, but more like Machiavelli's Prince, relying on the zigzagging path of masquerade and duplicity to achieve his ends. Schiller's story suggests – like those of G.K. Chesterton – that faith too has its cunning, however improper he makes it seem. Perhaps the last word goes to another prince (quoted by Schiller's), caught in an age tugged between Protestant and Catholic world-views, and thus exposed both to the temptations of ghosts (and spirits, and maybe Spirit) and to those of radical scepticism:

'There are more things in heaven and earth, Horatio,
Than are dreamt of in your philosophy.'
(*Hamlet* Act 1, Scene 5, ll 168–9)

– *Andrew Brown, 2003*

Note on the Text:

I have based this translation on the German text of Schiller's *Der Geisterseher und andere Erzählungen*, with an introduction by Emil Staiger and notes by Manfred Hoppe (Insel Verlag: Frankfurt am Main, 1976). I have also benefited from the translation published in the volume *Schiller's Early Dramas and Romances* (George Bell and Sons: London, 1881).

The Ghost-seer

Book One

I am going to recount an incident that will seem incredible to many, but of which I myself was to a large extent an eyewitness. The few people who are acquainted with a certain political event will find in this story – if indeed they are still alive to read these pages – a welcome explanation of it all; and even without this key, it will perhaps serve others as an important contribution to the history of the way the human mind can be deceived and go astray. Readers will be amazed at the boldness of objective which wickedness is capable of devising and prosecuting; they will be amazed at the strangeness of the means that it can muster to assure itself of this objective. Clear, unadorned truth will guide my pen; for by the time these pages appear in the world I will be no more and will have nothing to win or to lose from the report I am setting down.

It was on my return journey to Courland in the year 17** at carnival time when I was visiting the Prince of ** in Venice. We had got to know each other while serving in the army of **, and here renewed an acquaintance that peace had interrupted. As I in any case wished to see the most notable things in this city, and the Prince was merely waiting for bills of exchange to arrive so as to travel home to **, he easily persuaded me to keep him company and delay my departure for a while. We agreed not to separate for as long as our stay in Venice lasted, and the Prince was kind enough to suggest I share his own lodgings in the 'Moor'.

He was staying here under the strictest incognito, as he wanted to live independently, and his restricted allowance would not have permitted him to maintain the eminence of his rank. Two gentlemen on whose absolute discretion he could fully count, were, together with a few trusty servants, his only entourage. He avoided extravagance, more out of temperament than thrift. He shunned pleasures; at the age of thirty-five he had withstood all the allurements of this voluptuous city. The fair sex had until now remained a matter of indifference to him. Deep seriousness and a dreamy melancholy were the dominant tone of his character. His likes and dislikes drew no attention to themselves, but they were stubborn to an excessive degree; he formed attachments slowly and soberly, and his devotion was warm and permanent. In the midst of a noisy tumult of people he went on his way alone; locked up in his fantasy world, he was very often a stranger in the real one. No one was more innately prone to let himself be directed by others, although he was by no means weak. At the same time he was level-headed and reliable, once won over to a cause, and he had the courage both to combat one acknowledged prejudice and to die for another.

As the third prince of his house, he had no real prospect of ever reigning. His ambition had remained dormant, and his passions had taken another direction. Happy not to depend on the will of anyone else, he was not tempted to rule over others: the tranquil freedom of private life and a taste for intelligent company marked the limits of all his wishes. He read widely but indiscriminately; a neglected education and early service in the army had prevented his mind from maturing. All the knowledge that he picked up later on merely increased the confusion of his ideas, since they were built on no firm ground.

He was a Protestant, like his whole family – by birth, not by investigating the matter, which was something he had never done, even though at one period of his life he had been a religious enthusiast. He was, as far as I know, never a Freemason.

One evening, as we were strolling through St Mark's Square as we habitually did, completely disguised by our masks and isolated from the rest of the crowd – it was starting to get late and the press of people had dispersed – the Prince noticed that a masked man was following us wherever we went. It was an Armenian[1], walking along by himself. We started to walk more quickly and tried to throw off the masked man by frequently changing our route – but in vain: he stayed right behind us. 'You haven't by any chance become embroiled in a love affair here, have you?' the Prince finally asked me. 'Husbands in Venice can be dangerous.'

'I don't know a single lady in the place,' I replied.

'Let's sit down here and speak German,' he continued. 'I am starting to imagine we've been mistaken for someone else.'

We sat on a stone bench and waited for the masked man to walk past us. He immediately came right up to us and sat down next to the Prince. The latter took out his watch and said to me loud and clear, in French, as he rose to his feet: 'It's past nine o'clock. Come. We are forgetting that they are waiting for us in the "Louvre".' He said this merely so as to throw the masked man off our trail. '*Nine o'clock*,' the masked man repeated, again in French, emphatically and slowly. 'Congratulate yourself, Prince,' he added, calling the Prince by his real name. '*He died at nine o'clock*.' – Whereupon he stood up and left.

We looked at one another in consternation.

'Who has died?' the Prince finally asked, after a long silence.

'Let's follow him,' I said, 'and demand an explanation.'

We looked in every nook and cranny of St Mark's Square – the masked man was nowhere to be found. Feeling dissatisfied, we returned to our hotel. On the way, the Prince said not a word to me, but walked to one side, alone, seemingly profoundly agitated, as he later confessed to me was the case.

When we were back home, he opened his mouth for the first time. 'It is perfectly ridiculous,' he said, 'that a crazy man should be able to destroy one's peace of mind with two words.' We wished each other good night, and as soon as I was back in my room, I jotted down in my notebook the day and the time at which this had happened. It was a Thursday.

The following evening, the Prince said to me, 'Why don't we go for a walk across St Mark's Square and see if we can find our mysterious Armenian? I am longing to know how this comedy is going to turn out.' I was happy to do so. We stayed on the Square until eleven o'clock. The Armenian was nowhere to be seen. We did the same thing on the following four evenings, and met with no more success.

When we left our hotel on the sixth evening, I had the bright idea – whether involuntarily or deliberately, I cannot remember now – of leaving the servants with directions of where we could be found if anyone should ask after us. The Prince noticed my wise precaution and approved it with a smile. There was a dense throng on St Mark's Square when we arrived. We had hardly walked thirty paces when I again spotted the Armenian, speedily working his way through the crowd and apparently looking for someone. We were just about to reach him when the Baron von F** from the Prince's retinue came breathlessly up to us and handed the Prince a letter. 'It is sealed in black,' he added. 'We guessed that it must be urgent.' This was a veritable thunderclap for me. The Prince had stepped under a lamp and started to read. 'My cousin has died,' he exclaimed. '*When*?' I interrupted him, vehemently. He turned back to the letter. 'Last Thursday. At nine o'clock in the evening.'

We had no time to recover from our amazement for the Armenian was already standing among us. 'You have been recognised here, my lord,' he said to the Prince. 'Hurry back to the "Moor". There you will find the representatives of the Senate. Have no misgivings about accepting the honour that is to be shown you. The Baron von F** forgot to tell you that your bills of exchange have arrived.' He melted back into the crowd.

We hurried back to our hotel. There everything turned out to be just as the Armenian had announced. Three *nobili* of the Republic were standing ready to greet the Prince and accompany him with all pomp to the Assembly, where the aristocracy of the city were expecting him. He barely had enough time to convey to me, with a brief gesture, that I should sit up and wait for him.

At around eleven o'clock at night he returned. He came solemnly and pensively into the room and seized my hand, having dismissed the servants. 'Count,' he said, alluding to Hamlet's words: 'there are more things in heaven and earth than are dreamt of in our philosophies.'

'My lord,' I replied, 'you seem to be forgetting that you will be going to bed much richer in expectation.' (The deceased had been the heir to the throne, the only son of the reigning **, who was old and sickly and without hope of producing a new heir. An uncle of our Prince, also without heirs and without prospect of getting any, was now the only person standing between him and the throne. I mention this circumstance, as it will be cropping up again later on.)

'Do not remind me of it,' said the Prince. 'And even if a throne had been won for me, I would have more to do right now than brood over this trivial event. – If this Armenian has not simply guessed –'

'How would that be possible, Prince?' I cut in.

'Then you will see me exchange all my princely hopes for a monk's habit.'

The following evening we arrived earlier than usual in St Mark's Square. A sudden shower forced us to shelter in a coffee-house, where people were gambling. The Prince went and stood behind the chair of a Spaniard, and observed the game. I had gone into a neighbouring room where I read newspapers. A short while afterwards I heard a noise. Before the arrival of the Prince, the Spaniard had been losing repeatedly; now he was winning at every turn of the cards. The whole game had changed remarkably, and the bank was in danger of being required to pay up to the gambler who had been emboldened by this happy turn of events. The Venetian who kept the bank told the Prince in an insulting tone that he was disturbing the game and should leave the table. The Prince gazed at him coldly and stayed where he was; he maintained the same demeanour when the Venetian repeated his insult in French. The latter thought that the Prince could not understand either language, and turned with a contemptuous laugh to the others: 'So tell me then, gentleman, how am I to make myself understood to this bumpkin?' Whereupon he stood up and made as if to seize the Prince by the arm; the latter then lost patience, grabbed the Venetian with his strong hands and threw him roughly to the ground. The whole house was in uproar. Hearing the tumult, I rushed in, and instinctively called him by his name. 'Take care, Prince,' I added without thinking, 'don't forget we are in Venice.' The Prince's name imposed a general silence, from which soon arose a murmur that struck me as dangerous. All the Italians present crowded together into small groups, and stood to one side. One after the other they left the room, until the two of us were left alone with the Spaniard and a few Frenchmen. 'You are lost, my lord,' said the latter, 'unless you leave town immediately. The Venetian you have treated so badly is rich and of high standing – it will cost him a mere fifty sequins to get rid of you.' The Spaniard offered to fetch the guards to ensure the Prince's safety, and was even ready to accompany us home himself. The French were also willing to do the same. We were still standing there considering what to do when the door opened and several servants of the Inquisition entered. They showed us orders from the Government requesting us both to follow them immediately. Strongly guarded, we were led to the canal. Here a gondola was awaiting us, in which we were required to embark. Before we stepped out of it, our eyes were blindfolded. We were taken up a long stone flight of steps and then through a long winding corridor, over vaults, as I deduced from the multiple echo that resounded beneath our feet. Finally we came to another flight of twenty-six steps that led us downwards. The staircase opened onto a hall, in which our blindfolds were removed. We found ourselves in a circle of venerable old men, all dressed in black; the whole room was hung with black drapes and dimly lit, and there was a deathly hush in the whole gathering which made a fearful impression. One of the old men, presumably the senior State Inquisitor, approached the Prince and asked him solemnly, as the Venetian was brought up to him, 'Do you recognise this man as the same who insulted you in the coffee-house?'

'Yes,' replied the Prince.

Thereupon the Inquisitor turned to the prisoner: 'Is this the same person whom you intended to have murdered this evening?'

The prisoner replied yes.

Immediately the circle drew back, and we were horrified to see the Venetian's head being separated from his body. 'Are you satisfied with this amends?' asked the Inquisitor. – The Prince was lying in a faint in the arms of his escort. 'Now go,' continued the former with a dreadful voice, turning towards me, 'and in future be less hasty in your opinion of justice in Venice.'

Who the hidden friend had been who had availed himself of the quick arm of the law to save us from certain death, we could not guess. Dumbstruck with horror, we reached our residence. It was past midnight. The Chamberlain von Z** was impatiently waiting for us on the steps.

'What a good thing it was that you sent me a message!' he said to the Prince, lighting our way for us. 'The news that the Baron von F** brought home soon after from St Mark's Square had put us in a state of mortal fear for your safety.'

'I sent you a message? Why? I don't know a thing about it.'

'This evening, after eight o'clock. You sent us word that we shouldn't worry in the slightest if you came home later than usual this evening.'

At this point the Prince looked at me. 'Did you perhaps take this precaution without my knowledge?'

I knew nothing about it.

'But you must have done so, Your Highness,' said the chamberlain – 'for here is your repeating watch that you sent along as a guarantee.'

The Prince reached for his watch case. The watch really was missing, and he recognised the one held out as his own.

'Who brought it?' he asked in consternation.

'A stranger in a mask, wearing Armenian dress; he immediately went off again.'

We stood there, looking at one another. – 'What do you think of all this?' the Prince finally said after a long silence. 'There is a hidden guard keeping watch over me here in Venice.'

That night's dreadful scene made the Prince fall into a fever that obliged him to keep to his room for a week. During this time our hotel was swarming with people from Venice and abroad, all drawn by the Prince's newly revealed status. People vied with one another in offering their services to him, and each one tried in his own way to make himself useful. Our adventure with the Inquisition was not so much as mentioned. Since the Court of ** wished the Prince's departure to be further deferred, several money-changers in Venice received instructions to pay out considerable sums of money to him. So it was that he was, against his will, placed in the position of having to prolong his stay in Italy, and at his request I also decided to put off my departure for a while longer.

As soon as he was well enough again to be able to leave his room, the doctor persuaded him to take a trip along the Brenta and enjoy a change of air. The weather was fair, and the advice was accepted. Just as we were about to climb into the gondola, the Prince realised he had forgotten the key to a small casket that contained very important documents. We immediately turned back to fetch it. He clearly and distinctly remembered having locked the casket just the previous day, and since then he had not left his room. But however hard we looked, we could not find it; we had to give up our search so as not to lose time. The Prince, whose soul was too noble to harbour any suspicions, declared that it must be lost, and asked us not to mention it again.

The journey was as pleasant as could be. A picturesque landscape, which seemed to become richer and more beautiful at every twist and turn of the river; the clearest sky, that made mid-February seem more like a day in May; delightful gardens and countless tasteful houses adorning both banks of the Brenta; behind us, Venice in its majesty, with a hundred towers and masts stretching up from the water: all this presented us with the most splendid spectacle in the world. We abandoned ourselves completely to the magic of all this natural beauty, we were in the most serene of moods, the Prince himself lost his seriousness and vied with us in merry quips. Merry music resounded in our ears as we stepped out onto land a few Italian miles from the city. It came from a small village where just then a fair was being held; people of every kind were swarming around. A troupe of young girls and boys, in theatrical costume, welcomed us with a dance in mime. It was an inventive piece; lightness and grace animated every movement. Before the dance had quite ended, the girl leading it, dressed as a queen, suddenly seemed to have been gripped by an unseen arm. She stood there, motionless; so did everyone else. The music stopped. Not a breath could be heard in the whole gathering, and she stood there, staring fixedly at the ground, completely paralysed. All of a sudden she gave a start and, filled with fury like one inspired, looked wildly around her, cried 'A king is among us', tore her crown from her head, and laid it – at the Prince's feet. At this, everyone present turned to gaze at him, remaining uncertain for a long while as to whether there was any meaning behind this farce, so greatly had the affected seriousness of the actress deceived them. – A general burst of applause finally interrupted this silence. My eyes sought the Prince. I noticed that he was filled with consternation and making every attempt to evade the enquiring eyes of the spectators. He threw money for the children and started to make his way hastily through the throng.

We had gone just a few steps when a venerable barefooted friar forced his way through the crowd and stood in the Prince's way. 'Sir,' said the monk, 'give unto the Madonna of your riches, for you will be needing her prayers.' He said this in a tone of voice that made us feel abashed. He was jostled away by the crowd.

In the meantime our retinue had grown. An English lord, whom the Prince had already met in Nice, several merchants from Leghorn, a German canon, a French abbé with several ladies, and a Russian officer all joined us. The face of the latter had something quite unusual about it that drew our attention. Never in my life had I seen so many features and so little character, so much attractive benevolence with so much forbidding frostiness, all combined together in the face of one single human being. All the passions seemed to have left their ravages on it and then departed. There was nothing left but the quiet, penetrating gaze of a perfect connoisseur of human nature, who made everyone he met look away. This strange man followed us at a distance, but seemed to take but a negligent interest in everything that happened.

We found ourselves standing in front of a booth where lottery tickets were being drawn. The ladies joined in, and the others among us followed their example; even the Prince asked for a ticket. He won a snuffbox. As he was opening it, I saw him start back and turn pale. – The key was lying in it.

'What is all this?' the Prince said to me, when we were alone for a moment. 'A higher power is pursuing me. Some all-knowing shape is hovering around me. An invisible being from which I cannot escape is watching over my every step. I must track down the Armenian and get him to shed light on the subject.'

The sun was starting to set as we arrived outside the summer-house where the evening meal was being served. The Prince's name had swelled our entire company to sixteen persons. Apart from the ones I have already mentioned, we had now been joined by a virtuoso from Rome, a few Swiss men, and an adventurer from Palermo who was wearing a uniform and gave himself out as a captain[2]. It was decided that we would spend the entire evening here, and then go home by torchlight. The conversation at table was very animated, and the Prince could not help telling the story of the key, which aroused general astonishment. There was a vehement dispute on this subject. Most of the people there boldly explained it away, saying that all these occult arts could be attributed to sleight of hand; the abbé, who had already absorbed a fair quantity of wine, challenged the whole realm of ghosts to a duel; the Englishman uttered blasphemies; the musician made the sign of the cross to ward off the devil. A few, among them the Prince, were of the opinion that one should keep one's view of these things to oneself; meanwhile, the Russian officer was chatting to the ladies and seemed to be paying no attention at all to the conversation. In the heat of the dispute, no one had noticed that the Sicilian had left. After a short half hour he came back, wrapped in a cloak, and went and stood behind the Frenchman's chair. 'Just now you had the bravado to utter the wish that you might take on all the ghosts – do you want to try it with just *one*?'

'Agreed!' said the abbé, 'if you are prepared to take it upon yourself to get hold of one for me.'

'I am,' replied the Sicilian, turning towards us, 'if these ladies and gentlemen will please to leave us.'

'Whatever for?' cried the Englishman. 'A brave ghost is never afraid of a merry company.'

'I won't take responsibility for the outcome,' said the Sicilian.

'For heaven's sake! No!' shrieked the ladies round the table, and jumped up from their seats in alarm.

'Just let that ghost of yours come along,' said the abbé defiantly; 'but warn him first that there are some sharp blades waiting for him.' (Whereupon he asked one of the guests for his sword.)

'You can handle the matter any way you like,' replied the Sicilian coldly, 'if you are still in the mood for it.' Then he turned to the Prince. 'My lord,' he said to him, 'you stated that your key had been in someone else's hands. – Can you guess in whose?'

'No.'

'Is there nobody at all you can think of?'

'Well, there was of course one person I was thinking of…'

'Would you recognise that person if you could see them here before you?'

'Without a doubt.'

Then the Sicilian swept back his cloak and pulled out a mirror, which he held up to the Prince's eyes.

'Is this the person?'

The Prince stepped back in horror.

'Whom did you see?' I asked.

'The Armenian.'

The Sicilian stowed his mirror back under his cloak.

'Was that the person you had in mind?' everyone present asked the Prince.

'The very same.'

At this point every face changed expression, and the laughter died away. All eyes were fixed curiously on the Sicilian.

'Monsieur l'Abbé, things are getting serious,' said the Englishman; 'I'd think about beating a hasty retreat, if I were you.'

'That fellow is possessed by the devil,' cried the Frenchman, and ran out of the house; the ladies all rushed screaming from the room, the virtuoso followed them, the German canon was snoring away in an armchair, the Russian remained seated, just as indifferent as he had been all along.

'Maybe you just want to make a laughing-stock of a braggart,' the Prince began, once everyone else had left, 'or would you be so pleased as to keep your word to us?'

'It's true,' said the Sicilian. 'I wasn't being serious with the abbé – I made the proposal to him because I knew perfectly well that yellow-belly wouldn't take me at my word. – The matter is in any case much too serious merely to be the pretext for a practical joke.'

'So you admit that it is in your power?'

The sorcerer remained silent for a long while and seemed to be weighing up the Prince carefully with his gaze.

'Yes,' he finally said.

The Prince's curiosity was already aroused to the highest degree. To make contact with the ghost world had always been his most cherished dream, and ever since the Armenian's first appearance, all those ideas which his more mature reason had for so long dismissed had once more raised their heads. He took the Sicilian aside, and I heard him negotiating with him in tones of the greatest urgency.

'You see before you,' he continued, 'a man who is burning with impatience to reach some firm conviction on this important matter. I would embrace as my benefactor, as my best friend, the man who could here dispel my doubts and take the blindfold from my eyes – are you prepared to do me this great service?'

'What do you want from me?' asked the sorcerer, with some misgivings.

'For now, just a sample of your art. Let me see an apparition.'

'Where is that supposed to get you?'

'Then you will be able to judge, once you know me better, whether I am worthy of a higher level of instruction.'

'I esteem you above everything, my lord. A secret power lying in your face, of which you yourself are as yet unaware, bound me to you the moment I saw you. You are mightier than you yourself know. You can command all my powers, without reservation, – but –'

'Then let me see an apparition.'

'But I must first be sure that you are not making this demand of me out of mere curiosity. If indeed the invisible powers are to some degree at my beck and call, it is only on the hallowed condition that I do not profane hallowed secrets, that I do not misuse my talent.'

'My intentions are of the purest. I want the truth.'

Then they left the place where they were standing and walked over to a far window, where I could no longer hear them. The Englishman, who had also been listening in on this conversation, drew me aside.

'Your Prince is a man of noble character. I am sorry that he is getting mixed up with a confidence trickster.'

'It will all depend,' I said, 'on how the sorcerer gets himself out of it.'

'Do you know something?' said the Englishman, 'the wretched man is starting to name his price. He won't bother to demonstrate his art until he's heard the clink of cash. There are nine of us here. Let's make a collection and lead him into temptation by offering a high price. He'll come a cropper and the Prince's eyes will be opened.'

'That sounds good to me.'

The Englishman threw six guineas onto a plate and went round collecting more money. Everyone gave a few louis; the Russian in particular seemed in no small measure interested by our proposal, and placed a hundred-sequin banknote on the plate – an extravagance at which the Englishman expressed surprise. We brought the collection to the Prince. 'Be so kind,' the Englishman said, 'as to put in a word for us with that gentleman and ask him to let us see a sample of his art: we hope he will accept this small token of our appreciation.' The Prince placed a precious ring on the plate and handed it to the Sicilian. The latter considered it for a few moments.

'My lords and patrons,' he then began, 'this magnanimity puts me to shame. – I feel that you are misjudging me – but I will yield to your request. Your wish will be granted.' He pulled a bell. 'As far as this gold is concerned, to which I myself have no right, you will please allow me to give it away to the Benedictine monastery nearby as a donation for charitable purposes. This ring I will keep as a precious memento to remind me of the worthiest of princes.'

At this point the landlord came up, and the Sicilian immediately handed the money over to him.

'He's still a rogue,' the Englishman said in my ear. 'He's turning down the money because he's now much more interested in the Prince.'

'Or the landlord understands his instructions,' said another.

'Whom do you wish to call up?' the sorcerer now asked the Prince.

The Prince reflected for a moment. – 'Why not some great man?' called out the English lord. 'Call up Pope Ganganelli[3]. That won't cost the gentleman much.'

The Sicilian bit his lips. 'I must not summon anyone who has been consecrated.'

'That's a shame,' said the Englishman. 'We might perhaps have learnt from him what illness he died of.'

'The Marquis de Lanoy,' the Prince now broke in, 'was a French brigadier in the last war and my closest friend. At the battle of Hastinbeck he received a fatal wound, he was brought to my tent where he shortly afterwards died in my arms. When he was already in the throes of death, he motioned me to come over to him. "Prince," he began, "I will not see my fatherland again, and so let me tell you a secret to which no one apart from me has the key. In a convent on the Flemish border there lives a…" but at this point he died. The hand of death cut the thread of his narrative; I would like to have him brought hither so I can hear the rest of the story.'

'That's asking a lot, by God!' exclaimed the Englishman. 'I will hail you as a second Solomon if you can accomplish this task.'

We admired the Prince's sensible choice and gave it our unanimous approval. In the meantime the sorcerer paced energetically up and down, seemingly irresolute, and engaged in some inner struggle.

'And that was all the dying man had to tell you?'

'Yes, that was all.'

'Didn't you make any further enquiries on the subject in his fatherland?'

'They were all in vain.'

'Had the Marquis de Lanoy lived an irreproachable life? – I cannot call up just any dead man.'

'He died repenting the dissipations of his youth.'

'Do you carry on you anything to remember him by?'

'Yes.' (The Prince really did carry a snuffbox with him on which there was a miniature portrait of the marquis in enamel, and which he had placed next to him on the table.)

'I don't need to know what it is. – Leave me alone. You shall see the dead man.'

We were requested to take ourselves off to the other pavilion and wait there until he called us. Then he had all the furniture removed from the room, the windows taken out and the shutters closed as tightly as possible. He ordered the landlord, with whom he already seemed to be closely acquainted, to bring a vessel with burning coals and carefully extinguish with water all other fires in the house. Before we went away, he took from each of us in turn our word of honour that we would observe an eternal silence about what we would see and hear. After we had left, all the rooms in the pavilion behind us were bolted.

It was after eleven o'clock, and a deep silence reigned in the entire house. As we were going out, the Russian asked me whether we had loaded pistols with us.

'What for?' I said.

'Just in case,' he replied. 'Wait a moment, I'll go and look for some.'

He went away. The Baron von F** and I opened a window that looked across to the other pavilion, and we imagined we could hear two men whispering together, and a noise as if someone was setting a ladder against a wall. But this was just a guess on our part, and I cannot in all truth say whether it was really so. The Russian came back with a brace of pistols, having been away for half an hour. We saw him loading them with live ammunition. It was almost two o'clock when the sorcerer reappeared and announced to us that it was time. Before we went in, we were ordered to take our shoes off and appear in nothing but our shirts, stockings and underclothes. The doors were bolted after us as before.

When we came back into the room we found a broad circle had been drawn with a piece of coal, into which all ten of us could easily fit. All around, on the four sides of the room, the floorboards had been taken up so that we were, so to speak, standing on an island. An altar, draped with a black cloth, had been set up in the middle of the circle, and under it was stretched a red satin carpet. A Chaldee Bible lay open next to a death's-head on the altar, and on top of this a silver crucifix had been fastened. Instead of candles there was spirit oil burning in a silver vessel. A dense smoke of frankincense spread its dark vapours through the room and almost choked the flames. The sorcerer was half-dressed like us, but barefoot in addition; round his bare neck he was wearing an amulet on a chain made from human hair, and around his waist he had tied a white apron covered with mysterious ciphers and symbolic figures[4]. He told us to join hands, and observe a deep silence; he recommended in particular that we not put any questions to the apparition. He requested that the Englishman and I (for it was against us two that he seemed to harbour the deepest misgivings) hold steadily two naked swords crosswise an inch above the crown of his head for as long as the proceedings lasted. We stood in a half moon around him; the Russian officer placed himself right next to the Englishman and stood nearest to the altar. The sorcerer, his face turned to the east, now stood on the carpet, sprinkled holy water to all four corners and bowed three times before the Bible. The conjuration, of which we understood nothing, lasted a little more than five minutes. When he had finished, he signed to those standing immediately behind him that they should take a tight grip of his hair. Amid the most violent convulsions he called the dead man three times by his name, and the third time he stretched his hand out to the crucifix…

Suddenly we all simultaneously felt a blow like a thunderbolt, so violent that our hands fell apart; an abrupt clap of thunder shook the house, all the locks clattered, all the doors slammed to, the lid of the vessel fell shut, the light was extinguished, and on the opposite wall above the fireplace a human shape became visible, in a bloody shirt, pale, and with the face of a dying man.

'Who calls me?' said a hollow, barely audible voice.

'Your friend,' replied the sorcerer, 'who honours your memory and prays for your soul,' whereupon he gave the name of the Prince.

The answers always followed after a very long interval.

'What does he want?' the voice continued.

'He wishes to hear your confession to the end, the one you began in this world and never completed.'

'In a convent on the Flemish border there lives a –'

At this point the house trembled again. The door sprang open of its own volition at a violent clap of thunder, a flash of lightning lit up the room, and another bodily apparition, bloody and pale like the first, but more terrifying, appeared on the threshold. The spirit oil began to burn of its own accord, and the room became bright as it had been before.

'Who is among us?' cried the sorcerer in alarm, and darted a horrified glance through the assembly. '– I did not want *you*.'

The apparition went with majestic tread right up to the altar, stood on the carpet opposite us and grasped the crucifix. We could no longer see the first figure.

'*Who calls me?*' demanded this second apparition.

The sorcerer started to tremble violently. Fear and amazement held us spellbound. I reached for a pistol, the sorcerer tore it out of my hand and fired at the apparition. The bullet rolled slowly on the altar, and the apparition stepped quite unchanged out of the smoke. Then the sorcerer fell in a swoon.

'What's happening?' shouted the Englishman filled with amazement, and tried to strike the apparition with a sword. The apparition touched his arm, and the blade fell to the ground. A sweat broke out on my terrified brow. Baron von F** later confessed to us that he had been praying. Throughout this whole time, the Prince stood fearless and tranquil, his eyes fixed unmoving on the apparition.

'Yes! I recognise you,' he finally exclaimed with emotion, 'you are Lanoy, you are my friend. Whence do you come?'

'Eternity is mute. Ask me about my former life.'

'Who lives in the convent you told me about?'

'My daughter.'

'What? You were a father?'

'Woe is me, that I was too little a father!'

'Are you not happy, Lanoy?'

'God has judged me.'

'Can I still perform any service for you in this world?'

'None, other than to think of yourself.'

'How must I do that?'

'In Rome you will find out.'

Then there was another clap of thunder – a black cloud of smoke filled the room; when it had dispersed, the apparition had vanished. I forced open a shutter. It was morning.

The sorcerer was recovering from his faint. 'Where are we?' he cried, when he saw the light of day. The Russian officer was standing right behind him and gazing over his shoulder. '*Sorcerer*,' he said to him with a terrible look, '*you will never summon a ghost again.*'

The Sicilian turned round, looked him more closely in the face, uttered a loud cry, and fell at his feet.

Then we all at once looked at the supposed Russian. The Prince had no difficulty in recognising in him the features of his Armenian, and the words he tried to stammer out died on his lips. Fear and surprise had, as it were, turned us all to stone. In silence, immobile, we stared at this mysterious being, who in turn looked straight at us with a gaze of quiet power and grandeur. This silence lasted for a minute – and then another. There was not a breath to be heard in the whole gathering.

A violent battering on the door finally brought us back to ourselves. The door fell in pieces into the room, and several officers of justice, accompanied by a guard, pushed their way in. 'We're sure to find them together!' shouted the leader, and turned to his companions. 'In the name of the Government!' he shouted to us, 'you are all under arrest.' We did not have much time to gather our wits; in a few moments we were surrounded. The Russian officer, whom I will now call the Armenian, drew the chief officer aside and, insofar as I could make out in the confusion, I noticed that he said a few words in private in his ear and showed him a written paper. Immediately, the officer let him go, with a silent and respectful bow, turned to us and took off his hat. 'Forgive me, gentlemen,' he said, 'for mixing you up with this swindler. I will not ask who you are – but this gentleman assures me that I see men of honour before me.' With these words he motioned his companions to let go of us. He ordered the Sicilian to be closely guarded and tied up. 'It's high time we caught up with that fellow,' he added. 'We've already been after him for seven months.'

This wretched man was really an object of pity. The twofold horror of the second ghostly apparition and this unexpected arrest had quite overpowered his wits. He allowed himself to be tied up like a child; his eyes were wide open, staring and vacant in a face like a dead man's, and his lips were trembling and quivering mutely, unable to utter a single sound. At every moment we expected him to break down in convulsions. The Prince felt sympathy for the state he was in and undertook to effect his liberation from the chief officer, to whom he revealed his identity.

'My lord,' said the latter, 'do you really know for whom you are so magnanimously exerting yourself? The deception that he intended to perpetrate on you is the least of his crimes. We have his accomplices. They have terrible tales to tell of him. He can consider himself lucky if he gets off with the galleys.'

Meanwhile we also saw the landlord together with his staff, bound with a cord, being led across the courtyard. – 'He too?' cried the Prince. 'And what has *he* done wrong?'

'He was his accomplice and fence,' replied the chief officer. 'He helped him with his impostures and thefts and shared the booty with him. You will be convinced of this immediately, my lord.' With these words he turned to his companions. 'Search the whole house and let me know straight away what you find.'

Then the Prince looked round for the Armenian – but he was no longer there; in the general confusion caused by this incursion, he had found a way of making his escape unnoticed. The Prince was inconsolable; he forthwith wanted to send all his servants after him; he himself wanted to look for him, and drag me off with him. I hurried over to the window; the whole house was surrounded by a throng of curious onlookers, brought here by the rumour of these events. It was impossible to get through the crowd. I pointed this out to the Prince: 'If this Armenian is seriously intent on hiding from us, he is bound to know all the ins and outs better than we do, and all our investigations will be in vain. We'll do better to stay here, my lord. Perhaps this officer can tell us more about him, since the Armenian revealed his identity to him, if I indeed saw correctly.'

At this point we remembered that we were still in a state of undress.

We hurried back to our room and threw our clothes on in great haste. When we returned, the search of the house had been completed.

Once the altar had been moved away and the room's floorboards pulled up, a spacious vault had been uncovered, in which a man could sit comfortably upright; and a door led from it via a narrow flight of stairs to the cellar. In this vault, they found an electric machine, a clock, and a small silver bell, the last of which, like the electric machine, communicated with the altar and the crucifix fastened upon it. In a window shutter right opposite the fireplace an opening had been made into which a slide had been inserted, so as to make room for a magic lantern, from which the desired apparition had been projected onto the wall over the fireplace. From the attic and the cellar were brought various drums, from which lead balls attached by string were hanging, probably to produce the roar of thunder that we had heard. When the Sicilian's clothes were examined, they found in a small case various powders, as well as quicksilver in phials and tins, phosphorus in a glass bottle, a ring that we immediately recognised as magnetic, since it remained suspended from a steel button when it was brought up close to it, in the coat pockets a rosary, a Jew's beard, pistols and a dagger. 'Let's see if they are loaded!' said one of the officers, taking one of the pistols and aiming a shot into the fireplace. 'Jesus and Mary!' cried a hollow human voice, the same that we had heard coming from the first apparition – and in the same instant we saw a bleeding body come plunging down from the chimney. – 'Still not at rest, poor spirit?' exclaimed the Englishman while the rest of us jumped out of our skins with alarm. 'Go home to your grave. You appeared as what you were not; now you will be that which you appeared to be.'

'Jesus and Mary! I'm wounded,' repeated the man in the fireplace. The ball had smashed his right leg. Steps were immediately taken to have the wound bandaged.

'So who are you, and what kind of evil demon brings you here?'

'A poor barefooted friar,' the wounded man replied. 'A strange gentleman gave me a sequin, so I would…'

'Say the magic words? And why then didn't you clear off as soon as you'd done so?'

'He was going to give me a sign when it was time for me to go, but the

23

sign never came, and when I tried to climb out, the ladder had been taken away.'

'And how do the magic words go – the ones he taught you to say?'

At this point the man fell into a swoon, and we could get nothing further out of him. When we examined him more closely, we recognised him as the one who had stood in the Prince's way the evening before and spoken so solemnly to him.

In the meantime, the Prince had turned to the chief officer.

'You have,' he said, pressing a few gold coins into his hand, 'saved us from the wiles of an impostor and, even before knowing who we were, dealt justly with us. Will you now give us even more cause for gratitude and disclose to us the identity of the stranger who merely had to utter a few words for us to be set free?'

'Whom do you mean?' asked the chief officer, with an expression on his face that clearly indicated how needless this question was.

'I mean the man in Russian uniform who just now took you aside, showed you a written paper and spoke a few words in your ear, whereupon you immediately released us.'

'So you don't know this gentleman?' the officer again asked. 'He wasn't one of your company?'

'No,' said the Prince, '– and I have very important reasons to wish to become more closely acquainted with him.'

'But I am not well acquainted with him myself,' answered the officer. His very name is unknown to me, and today is the first time in my life that I've seen him.'

'What? And in such a short time, with just a few words, he was able to exert enough influence over you to convince you that both he, and all of us, were innocent?'

'Not with a few words: just one.'

'And what was that word? – I confess that I'd really like to know.'

'This stranger, my lord,' said the officer, weighing the sequins in his hand, 'was – you have been too generous to me for me to keep it secret from you any more – this stranger was – an officer of the Inquisition.'

'The Inquisition! – That man!'

'No other, my lord – and the thing that convinced me of the fact was the paper that he showed me.'

'That man, you said? It is not possible.'

'I can tell you even more, my lord. It was this very man who had made the denunciation which led to my being sent here yesterday to arrest the sorcerer.'

We looked at one another in even greater amazement.

'That,' the Englishman finally exclaimed, 'would be the explanation of why the poor devil of a sorcerer jumped out of his skin with shock when he looked more closely at his face. He recognised that he was a spy, and that's the reason he uttered that cry and fell at his feet.'

'Never,' cried the Prince. 'This man is everything he claims to be, and everything the moment requires him to be. What he really is, no mortal has ever yet known. Did you see the Sicilian slump, when he shouted into his ear: "*You will never summon a ghost again!*" There is more to this than meets the eye. No one will ever persuade me that it is usual to show such terror in the face of a merely human threat.'

'The sorcerer himself will be the best person to put us to rights about that,' said the English lord, 'if this gentleman' – and here he turned to the chief officer – 'will give us an opportunity to speak to his prisoner.'

The chief officer promised that he would, and we arranged with the Englishman that we would come and fetch him the very next morning. Then we made our way back to Venice. At daybreak Lord Seymour (this was the Englishman's name) arrived and was shortly afterwards followed by a confidant sent by the chief officer to conduct us to the prison. I had forgotten to mention that the Prince had for some days now been missing one of his footmen, an inhabitant of Bremen, who had served him honestly for many years and had gained his fullest confidence. Whether he had met with an accident, or been abducted, or even run away, nobody knew. But there was absolutely no plausible reason to suppose the latter, since he had at all times been a quiet, orderly man and had never incurred the slightest reproach. The only thing his comrades could think of was that he had lately been very melancholy and, whenever he could find a spare moment, he had visited a certain Minorite friary in the Giudecca where he frequently associated with some of the brothers. This led us to surmise that he had perhaps fallen into the hands of the monks and turned Catholic; and since the Prince at that time was still quite indifferent on this issue, he was content to carry out a few investigations that remained fruitless. But he was pained by the loss of this man, who had been at his side on all his campaigns, had always followed him faithfully, and was not so easy to replace in a foreign country. On that particular day, just as we were about to go out, the Prince's banker was announced, who had been given the job of finding a new servant. He introduced to the Prince a well-educated and elegantly dressed man in middle age who had long worked as the secretary of a procurator; he spoke French and even a little German, and, what is more, he came with the best references. The Prince liked his face, and as, furthermore, the newcomer made it clear that his salary could depend on the extent to which his services met with the Prince's satisfaction, he took him on forthwith.

We found the Sicilian in a private cell, to which he had been brought temporarily, for the Prince's benefit, so the court officer said, before being taken to the Piombi or 'lead roofs', to which no access is granted. These Piombi are the most dreadful prison in Venice, situated under the roof of the St Mark's Square palace; in them, the unhappy criminals are often made quite delirious by the blazing heat of the sun that falls full on the lead roofs. The Sicilian had recovered from all that had chanced the day before and stood up respectfully when the Prince appeared. One leg and one arm were bound in chains, but apart from that he was free to move around the room. On our entrance the guard withdrew outside the door.

'I come,' said the Prince, once we had sat down, 'to ask you for an explanation of two points. You owe me an explanation for the one, and it will do you no harm to satisfy me as regards the other.'

'My role is played out,' the Sicilian replied. 'My fate stands in your hands.'

'Your honesty alone,' replied the Prince, 'can mitigate it.'

'Ask away, my lord. I am ready to answer, for I have nothing more to lose.'

'You showed the Armenian's face in your mirror. How did you manage to do that?'

'It wasn't a mirror that you saw. A mere pastel painting behind glass, representing a man in Armenian costume, deceived you. The speed with which I showed it to you, the twilight, your amazement, all

26

fostered this illusion. The picture will be found with the other things that have been confiscated in the hotel.'

'But how were you able to know my thoughts so exactly, and hit upon the Armenian?'

'But this wasn't all that difficult, my lord. Without doubt you often dropped a few remarks at table, in the presence of your servants, touching on what had happened between you and this Armenian. One of my servants struck up a chance acquaintance in the Giudecca with a footman in your service; he gradually managed to draw from him all that I needed to know.'

'Where is this footman?' asked the Prince. 'I miss him, and you certainly know of his defection.'

'I swear to you that I don't know the slightest thing about it, my lord. I myself have never seen him and never had anything else to do with him other than what I have just told you.'

'Carry on then,' said the Prince.

'Well, in this way I also received the first news of your stay in Venice and what had befallen you there, and I immediately decided to make use of what I had learnt. You can see, my lord, that I am being sincere. I knew about your planned excursion on the Brenta; I had made provision for it, and a key that you chanced to drop gave me the first opportunity to try my art on you.'

'What? So I was wrong? That bit of business with the key was your doing, and not the Armenian's? I dropped the key, you say?'

'Yes, when you took out your wallet – and I spotted the opportunity, as nobody was watching me, to cover it quickly with my foot. The person from whom you bought the lottery tickets was in league with me. He ensured the number was drawn from a barrel that contained no blanks, and the key had been lying in the snuffbox long before it could be won by you.'

'Now I understand. And the barefoot friar who threw himself in my way and spoke to me so solemnly?'

'– was the same who, I hear, was pulled wounded out of the fireplace. He is one of my comrades who has already served me well on several occasions in this disguise.'

'But what was the purpose of all this?'

'To make you thoughtful – to prepare in you a frame of mind that would make you receptive to the marvel I intended to show you.'

'But the dance in mime that took such a strange and surprising turn – this at least was not your fabrication?'

'The girl who was playing the queen had been instructed by me, and her whole performance was my work. I guessed that Your Highness would be in no small measure surprised if you were recognised in that place, and – forgive me, my lord – the adventure with the Armenian gave me the hope that you would already be inclined to spurn natural explanations and seek a higher source for those extraordinary happenings.'

'Indeed,' cried the Prince, with a look of simultaneous annoyance and astonishment. 'Indeed,' he exclaimed, 'I hadn't expected *that*. But,' he continued, after a long silence, 'how did you produce the apparition that appeared on the wall over the fireplace?'

'Through the magic lantern that had been fitted into the opposite window shutter – you will have noticed the opening.'

'But how did it happen that not a single one of us spotted it?' asked Lord Seymour.

'You will remember, my lord, that when you returned to the room a thick smoke was casting its pall throughout it. I had also taken the precaution of having the floorboards that had been taken up placed against the same window where the Lanterna Magica had been fitted; in this way I prevented your eyes from falling directly on that shutter. In addition, the lantern remained hidden behind a slide until you had all taken your places and there was no further fear of you examining the room.'

'It seemed to me,' I broke in, 'as if I could hear a ladder being set up near this room as I was looking out of the window in the other pavilion. Was that really the case?'

'Quite so. It was the very same ladder my assistant climbed up to the window in question, so as to direct the magic lantern.'

'The apparition,' continued the Prince, 'really did seem to have a fleeting resemblance to my dead friend – in particular, its extremely blond hair was very like his. Was this mere coincidence, or how did you find out about it?'

'Your Highness will remember that at table you had placed a snuffbox next to you, on which the portrait of an officer in the uniform of the ** army was depicted in enamel. I asked you whether by chance you carried a memento of your friend with you; whereupon you answered yes. From that I guessed that it might well be the snuffbox. I had gazed closely at the picture over the table, and as I am an experienced drawer, and very good at catching people's likeness, it was an easy thing for me to give to the apparition that fleeting resemblance that you remarked on; all the more so, as the features of the Marquis are most striking.'

'But the apparition seemed to move –'

'So it appeared – but it wasn't the apparition, but the smoke, that was lit up by its gleam.'

'And so it was the man who fell down the chimney who answered on behalf of the apparition?'

'The very same.'

'But surely he couldn't hear the questions very well.'

'He didn't need to. You will remember, my lord, that I forbade you all in the strictest terms from asking the ghost even a single question. What I would ask him, and what he would reply, had been arranged beforehand; and so that there would be no mistake, I had him observe long pauses, which he had to count by the ticking of a clock.'

'You gave the landlord the order to have all fires in the house carefully extinguished with water; this doubtless happened –'

'… so as to ensure my man in the fireplace wouldn't run the risk of choking, as the chimneys in the house all run together, and I didn't think I was entirely safe from your retinue.'

'But how was it,' asked Lord Seymour, 'that your ghost appeared on the scene neither sooner nor later than you needed him to be?'

'My ghost had already been in the room for quite a while before I summoned him; but as long as the spirit oil was burning, his faint gleam could not be seen. When my formula of conjuration was finished, I let the lid of the vessel in which the spirit oil was flickering fall shut, the room was plunged into darkness, and only then did people become aware of the figure on the wall that had already been reflected on it for a considerable time.'

'But at the very same moment the ghost appeared, we all felt an electric shock. How did you contrive that?'

'You discovered the machine under the altar. You also saw that I was standing on a silken rug. I got you all to stand in a half moon round me and hold hands; just before the crucial moment, I motioned one of you to take a grip of my hair. The crucifix was the conductor, and you experienced the shock when I touched it with my hand.'

'You ordered us – Count von O** and myself –' said Lord Seymour, 'to hold two naked swords crosswise over the crown of your head for as long as the conjuration would last. What was this for?'

'It had no other purpose than that of keeping you both busy throughout the whole act, as you were the ones I least trusted. You will remember that I expressly told you to hold them an inch over my head; since you would have to pay close attention to this distance, you were prevented from directing your gaze where I didn't want you to look. I had not yet become aware of my worst enemy.'

'I must confess,' cried Lord Seymour, 'this was all planned with great care – but why did we have to take some of our clothes off?'

'Merely to give the proceedings added solemnity and to enable their unusual character to rouse your powers of imagination.'

'The second apparition didn't let your ghost speak,' said the Prince. 'What were we actually supposed to learn from him?'

'More or less the same as you heard later. It was on purpose that I asked Your Highness whether you had told me everything the dying man had entrusted to you, and whether you had not carried out further investigations on the subject in his homeland; I found this necessary so I wouldn't come up against facts that might have contradicted the statements made by my ghost. It was certain youthful peccadilloes I had in mind when I asked whether the dead man had led an irreproachable life, and I then based my fabrication on the answer.'

'On this matter,' began the Prince, after a brief silence, 'you have given me a satisfactory explanation. But there is one essential circumstance that I would like you to shed light on for me.'

'If it is in my power, and –'

'No conditions! The judicial system in whose hands you find yourself wouldn't interrogate you so gently. Who was that stranger at whose feet we saw you fall? What do you know about him? How do you know him? And what is the link with that second apparition?'

'My lord –'

'When you looked him more closely in the face, you uttered a loud cry and fell down. Why? What was the meaning of that?'

'That stranger, my lord –' He paused, became visibly more disquieted, and looked round at us all, one after the other, with embarrassment in his eyes. 'Yes, by God, my lord, that stranger is a terrible being.'

'What do you know about him? What is the nature of his relationship to you? Don't imagine you can conceal the truth from us.'

'I will take good care that I don't – for who can guarantee that he isn't standing among us this very minute?'

'Where? Who?' we all exclaimed at once, and looked round the room, half laughing and half disturbed. '– But that is quite impossible.'

'Oh! For this man – or whatever he may be – things are possible that are even more incomprehensible.'

'But who is he, then? Where does he come from? Is he Armenian or Russian? What truth is there in the identity he gives himself?'

'There is no truth in any of his appearances. There are few classes, characters and nations whose mask he has not already worn. Who is he, you ask? Where does he come from? Where is he going? Nobody knows. That he spent a long time in Egypt, as many people assert, and gained his hidden wisdom from one of the pyramids, I will neither affirm nor deny. Among us he is known only under the name of *The Unfathomable*. How old do you think he is, for instance?'

'Judging from his external appearance, he can't be much more than forty.'

'And how old do you think *I* am?'

'Not far off fifty.'

'Quite right – and if I now tell you that I was a boy of seventeen when my grandfather told me of this man of marvels, whom he saw in Famagusta looking about the same age as he does now –'

'That is ridiculous, incredible, and exaggerated.'

'Not a bit of it. If I weren't prevented by these chains, I would give you guarantees of such venerable and trustworthy quality that you would be left with no more doubts. There are reliable people who recall having seen him in various parts of the world, each at the same time. No sword's point can pierce him, no poison harm him, no fire burn him, no ship ever sinks if he is on board. Time itself seems to lose its power over him, the years do not dry up his vital juices, and old age cannot whiten his hair. There is nobody who has even seen him take food, no woman has ever been touched by him, no sleep ever visits his eyes; in all the hours of the day, people know of only a single one over which he is not master – an hour at which nobody has ever seen him and he has never done any earthly business.'

'Is that so?' said the Prince. 'And what hour is that?'

'The twelfth hour of night. As soon as the bell tolls for the twelfth time, he no longer belongs among the living. Wherever he may be, he must away, whatever business he is engaged in, he must break it off. This dreadful stroke of the bell tears him out of the arms of friendship, even tears him away from the altar, and would summon him even from his death throes. No one knows where he then goes, or when there, what he gets up to. No one dares to ask him, let alone to follow him, for as soon as this dreaded hour strikes, his features immediately tense up into an expression of such a sombre and anxious seriousness that no one has the courage to look into his face or speak to him. A deep and deadly silence then suddenly brings the liveliest conversation to a halt, and all those around him wait in deferential trembling for his return, without even daring to rise from their seats or to open the door through which he left.'

'But,' one of our party asked, 'is there nothing out of the ordinary to be seen in him when he returns?'

'Nothing, except that he appears pale and exhausted, somewhat like a man who has undergone a painful operation or has just received some dreadful news. Some claim they have seen drops of blood on his shirt, but that is a question I leave open.'

'And has no one ever tried at least to conceal the time from him, or to catch his attention in something so complex that he becomes absent-minded and overlooks it?'

'On one single occasion, it is said, he exceeded the deadline. The company was numerous, people were staying on until late in the night, all the clocks had been carefully set to tell the wrong time, and the heat of the discussion carried him away. When the ordained time came, he suddenly fell silent and stiffened, all his limbs froze in the very position in which this sudden and unexpected turn of events found them, his eyes stood out, his pulse stopped, all the means deployed to reawaken him were fruitless; and this state of affairs persisted until the hour had elapsed. Then he suddenly and spontaneously came back to life, opened his eyes and continued speaking from the very syllable at which he had been interrupted. The general consternation told him what had happened, and he then declared with fearful seriousness that they should all think themselves lucky they had got away with nothing worse than a fright. But that very same evening he left forever the city in which this had happened. The general belief is that in this mysterious hour he discourses with his genius. Indeed, a few claim that he is a dead man to whom it has been granted to walk abroad among the living for twenty-three hours a day, while in the last hour his soul has to return to the underworld, so as to endure the punishment imposed on it. Many others consider that he is the celebrated Apollonius of Tyana[5], and yet others think he is St John the Apostle, of whom it is said that he would remain until the Last Judgement.'

'Bold surmises,' said the Prince, 'can of course hardly fail to arise in the case of an extraordinary man. Everything you have said until now is merely a matter of hearsay; and yet his behaviour towards you, and yours towards him, seemed to me to indicate a closer acquaintance. Isn't there some particular story at the bottom of all this – one in which you yourself have been involved? Keep nothing back from us.'

The Sicilian looked at us with eyes full of doubt and said nothing.

'If it concerns a matter,' continued the Prince, 'that you are unwilling to make public, then I can assure you in the name of both these gentlemen of our most absolute discretion. But tell us your story honestly and openly.'

'If I can really count on you not to use this in evidence against me,' the man commenced after a long silence, 'I will indeed tell you of a remarkable event involving this Armenian, one of which I was an eyewitness and which will leave you with no further doubts as to the hidden power of this man. But I must be permitted,' he added, 'to conceal some of the names in the story.'

'Is there no way round this stipulation?'

'No, my lord. It involves a family that I have reason not to involve in all this.'

'Let us hear all about it,' said the Prince.

'It must be a good five years ago now,' began the Sicilian, 'that I was in Naples, practising my art with reasonable success, and made the acquaintance of a certain Lorenzo del M**nte, Chevalier of the Order of St Stephen, a rich young gentleman from one of the foremost families in the kingdom who showered me with civilities and seemed to hold the mysteries of my art in the greatest esteem. He disclosed to me that the Marchese del M**nte, his father, was a zealous devotee of the cabbala, and would count himself fortunate to have a man of worldly wisdom (as he liked to call me) staying under his roof. The old man lived in one of his country estates by the sea, about seven miles from Naples, where in almost total seclusion from others he lamented the memory of a dear son who had been torn from him by a dreadful fate. The Chevalier gave me to understand that he and his family might well one day need my help with a very serious matter, where I could perhaps use my secret science to unearth a piece of information about something which they had exhausted all natural means in trying to discover, without success. He in particular, he added significantly, would perhaps eventually have reason to consider me as the man who ensured his peace of mind and his whole earthly happiness. I did not dare question him about this more closely, and for the time being he went no further in his explanations. But this is how it all fell out:

'This Lorenzo was the Marchese's younger son, and for that reason he was also destined for a career in the Church; the family's wealth was to fall to his elder brother. Jeronymo, for such was the name of this elder brother, had spent several years travelling, and returned to his father-land about seven years before the events I am relating, to formalise a marriage with the only daughter of a neighbouring family, that of the Count of C**tti, which had been arranged by these two families ever since the birth of these children, so as to unite their considerable wealth. Despite the fact that this liaison was simply for their parents' convenience, and the hearts of the two concerned had not been consulted on the choice, they had nonetheless already tacitly confirmed it. Jeronymo del M**te and Antonia C**tti had been brought up together, and the relative lack of compulsion that was imposed on the contacts between two children who were already habitually considered as a couple, had early allowed a tender mutual understanding to blossom between them; it was made even stronger by the harmony of their characters and, as soon as they were mature enough, it ripened into true love. An absence of four years had made them grow fonder rather than cooling their ardour, and Jeronymo returned just as faithful and just as fiery to the arms of his bride as if he had never torn himself away from her embrace.

'The ecstasies of their reunion were still unabated, and the preparations for the marriage were being made in the briskest fashion, when the bridegroom – disappeared. He was often in the habit of spending entire evenings in a country house that looked out over the sea, and would occasionally indulge himself by going out sailing while he was there. After one such evening, it happened that he stayed out unusually late. Messengers were dispatched after him, vessels were sent out to sea to search for him; nobody could find any trace of him. None of his servants was missing, so he couldn't have taken any with him. Night fell, and he still did not appear. Morning came – midday and evening, and still no Jeronymo. People were already starting to resign themselves to the worst when news came in that an Algerian corsair had landed on that coast the previous day, and several of the inhabitants had been captured and led away. Immediately, two galleys that were ready to sail were manned; the old Marchese himself boarded the one, resolving to free his son at the risk of his own life. On the third morning they caught sight of the corsair, and the wind gave them the advantage; they had soon caught up with it, and came so close that Lorenzo, who was on board the first galley, thought he recognised a sign of his brother on the enemy's deck, when a storm suddenly drove them apart. The ships, though damaged, just managed to come through it; but their prize had vanished, and they were compelled to land on Malta. The family's sorrow knew no bounds; the inconsolable old Marchese tore out his steely-grey hair, and people feared for the life of the young Countess.

'Five years went by in fruitless investigations. Enquiries were made along all the coasts of Barbary; huge rewards were offered for the young Marchese's freedom; but no one turned up to claim the prize. Finally, they came to the conclusion that the storm which had separated the two vessels had probably sunk the robbers' ship and its entire crew had lost their lives in the waves.

'However plausible this supposition might be, too many facts were missing to convert it into a certainty, and nothing justified the complete abandonment of the hope that the lost man might one day reappear. But if it were the case that he would never return, the family would die out with him, unless the second brother renounced his career in the Church and assumed the rights of the first-born. However bold this step and however unjust it was in itself to deprive the brother who was possibly still alive of his natural rights, it was thought that this eventuality was so unlikely that it did not constitute grounds for risking the fate of an ancient and brilliant lineage that would perish unless these arrangements were made. Grief and age were bringing the old Marchese ever nearer the grave; with every new search that produced no results, the hope of finding his lost son diminished. He could foresee the ruin of his house unless it could be prevented by committing a minor injustice – if he would only resolve to favour the younger brother at the expense of the elder. To fulfil the obligations he had contracted towards the family of the Count of C**tti, it merely required a name to be changed; the purpose of both families was achieved either way, whether Countess Antonia was the wife of Lorenzo or of Jeronymo. The faint *possibility* that the latter would reappear was of no importance when compared with the *certain* and impending evil of the complete ruin of his family, and the old Marchese, who sensed the approach of death more strongly every day, was filled with the impatient wish to die free from *this* anxiety at least.

'The only person to prevent this step and show himself most stubbornly opposed to it was the one who stood to win most from it – Lorenzo. Unaffected by the lure of immeasurable wealth, and even insensible to the possession of the most lovable creature who was to be delivered into his arms, he refused with the most magnanimous conscientiousness to rob a brother who was perhaps still alive and might claim his property back. "Is not the fate of my dear Jeronymo," he said, "already terrible enough through his long imprisonment, without my making it even more bitter through a theft that deprives him of all that he held most dear? With what emotions in my heart could I implore Heaven for his return if his wife were to lie in my arms? With what expression on my face would I hurry to meet him if finally some miracle restored him to us? And even if he has been torn from us forever, how better can we honour his memory than by leaving the hole that his death has rent in our circle forever unfilled? Or by sacrificing all our hopes on his grave and leaving what was his untouched, like a holy relic?"

'But all the arguments which his brotherly delicacy could adduce were unable to reconcile the old Marchese to the idea of seeing die out a family-tree that had flourished for centuries. The only concession Lorenzo could win from him was a period of grace of two years, before he led his brother's bride to the altar. During this period, investigations were continued in the most assiduous way. Lorenzo himself embarked on several sea voyages, and exposed his own person to many a danger; no effort, no expense was spared in the quest for the lost man. But these two years also went by as fruitlessly as all the preceding ones.'

'And what about Countess Antonia?' asked the Prince. 'You haven't told us anything about the state she was in. Was she supposed to yield so gently to her fate? I cannot believe it.'

'Antonia's state of mind was the most dreadful struggle between duty and passion, repulsion and admiration. The selfless magnanimity of Jeronymo's brother's love touched her; she felt impelled to honour the man she could never love; torn apart by conflicting emotions, her heart bled. But her aversion to the Chevalier seemed to grow in exact proportion as his claims on her esteem grew. With deep sorrow he saw the silent grief that was consuming her youth. A delicate empathy surreptitiously replaced the indifference with which he had hitherto considered her, but this treacherous feeling deceived him, and a violent passion soon made it difficult for him to execute a duty that had up until now vanquished every temptation. Yet even if it meant cheating his heart of its desires, he still heeded the dictates of his generous spirit; he alone it was who took the unhappy victim under his wing against the arbitrary rulings of his family. All his exertions failed, however: every victory that he won over his passion merely proved that he was all the worthier of her, and the magnanimity with which he repressed his feelings merely served to leave her with no excuse for resistance.

'So things stood, when the Chevalier persuaded me to visit him on his country estate. The warm recommendation of my patron ensured me of a welcome that exceeded all my expectations. I must not forget to remark at this point that I had succeeded through various conspicuous achievements in making quite a name for myself in the Masonic lodges there, and this had perhaps contributed to increasing the old Marchese's trust, and given him heightened expectations of me. Permit me not to divulge the lengths to which I went with him, and the means I employed; from the confession I have already made to you, you can deduce all the rest. As I took advantage of all the mystical books that were to be found in the Marchese's extremely well-stocked library, I was soon able to converse with him in his own language and bring my system of the invisible world into harmony with his own opinions. In a short while he believed what I wanted him to believe, and he would have sworn to the copulations of the philosophers with salamanders and sylphs just as confidently as if he were swearing to an article in the creed. As he was, furthermore, very religious, and his predisposition to belief had developed to a high degree in this school, my fairy stories found an even easier way into his acceptance, and in the end I had so entangled and ensnared him in a mystical maze that nothing merely natural now met with any credence on his part. In short, I was the venerated apostle of the household. The usual subject of my lectures was the exaltation of human nature and the communication of men with higher beings; my source was the infallible *Comte de Gabalis*[6]. The young Countess, who ever since the loss of her beloved had lived more in the world of ghosts than in the real world and was drawn with passionate fascination to objects of this kind through the fervent and fanciful flights of her imagination, seized with tremulous satisfaction on the hints I dropped before her; even the household servants tried to be present in the room when I spoke so as here and there to catch a word or two of mine, which fragments they immediately passed on to one another in their own way.

'I must have spent about two months in this country estate when one morning the Chevalier stepped into my room. Deep sorrow was depicted on his face, all his features were convulsed, and he flung himself into a chair with all the gestures of despair.

' "Captain," he said, "it is all up with me. I must get away. I cannot stand it any longer."

' "What is the matter with you, Chevalier? What is wrong?"

' "Oh, this dreadful passion!" (At this point he vehemently rose from the chair and flung himself into my arms.) "– I have struggled against it manfully. – I cannot resist it any longer."

' "But who decides that, my dearest friend, apart from yourself? Is not everything in your power? Father, family –"

' "Father! Family! What is all that to me? – Do I want to win her hand through compulsion, or through her free inclination? – Do I not have a rival? – Ah! And what a rival? A rival among the dead, perhaps? Oh let me go! Let me go! Even if it should mean going to the ends of the earth. I must find my brother."

' "What? After so many failed attempts, you can still hold out a hope – "

' "Hope! – In *my* heart, hope died long ago. But in hers? – What does it matter whether or not *I* hope? – Can I be happy as long as there is still a glimmer of this hope in Antonia's heart? – Two words, friend, could end my torment. – But in vain! My fate will remain wretched until eternity breaks its long silence and the graves bear witness on my behalf."

' "So only this certainty can make you happy?"

' "Happy? Oh, I doubt whether I can ever be happy again! – But uncertainty is the most terrible damnation!" (After a short silence he managed to control himself and continued in a melancholy tone.) "If only he could see my sufferings! – Can that constancy of hers make him happy when it makes his brother so wretched? Must a living man languish because of a dead man who can no longer taste life's joy? – If he knew my torment –" (at this point he began to sob, and pressed his face against my chest) "perhaps – yes, perhaps he himself would lead her to my arms."

' "But must this wish remain so unfulfillable?"

' "Friend! What are you saying?" – He looked at me in fear and amazement.

' "Far lesser occasions," I continued, "have interwoven the departed into the fate of the living. Should the entire earthly happiness of a man – a brother –"

' "The entire earthly happiness! Oh, that is what I feel! How truly you have spoken! My entire felicity!"

' "And might not the peace of mind of a grieving family be a legitimate reason for summoning up invisible powers to their aid? But of course! If any earthly occasion can ever be a justifiable cause for disturbing the peace of the blessed – to use a power –"

' "For God's sake, friend!" he interrupted me, "not a word more. Once upon a time, I confess, I nursed such a thought – I think I mentioned it to you – but I have long rejected it as dastardly and loathsome."

'You will have guessed already,' continued the Sicilian, 'where this all led us. I took pains to dissipate the reservations of the Chevalier and finally succeeded. It was decided to call up the ghost of the dead man, for which I required merely a fortnight's notice, in order, as I pretended, to prepare myself in a worthy manner for it. Once this period had elapsed and my machines were properly set up, I availed myself of one gloomy evening when the family was as usual gathered round me, to obtain their consent, or rather to coax them imperceptibly to the point where they themselves made the request of me. The most difficult one to convince was the young Countess, whose presence was nonetheless so essential; but here the dreamy and enthusiastic flight of her passion came to our aid, and even more, perhaps, a feeble glimmer of hope that the man believed to be dead might still be alive and would not appear when summoned. Lack of confidence in the actual procedure, or doubts about my art, were the one hindrance that I *didn't* have to contend with.

'As soon as the family had given their consent, the third day was fixed for the conjuration. Prayers that had to be continued until midnight, fasting, vigils, solitude and mystical instruction, together with the use of a certain as yet unknown musical instrument that in such cases I found particularly effective[7], constituted the preparations for this solemn act – preparations that turned out so much as I had wished that the fanatical enthusiasm of my listeners stoked the fire of my own imagination and in no small measure heightened the illusion that on this occasion I had to strive to produce in myself. Finally, the long-awaited hour came –'

'I can guess,' cried the Prince, 'whom you are going to introduce us to now. – But go on – go on –'

'No, my lord. The conjuration passed off as desired.'

'What? Where's the Armenian got to?'

'Don't worry,' replied the Sicilian, 'the Armenian will appear only too soon.

'I won't get involved in a description of the farce, as it would in any case lead me too far afield. Suffice it to say that it fulfilled all my expectations. The old Marchese, the young Countess with her mother, the Chevalier and a few other relatives were present. You will easily imagine that, throughout the long time I had spent in this house, opportunities had not been lacking for me to make the most detailed enquiries on everything concerning the deceased. Various portraits of him that I came across put me in the position of being able to give the apparition the most deceptive similarity to him, and as I allowed the ghost to speak only in signs, his voice would not be able to awaken any suspicions. The dead man himself appeared in the clothes of a slave from the Barbary coast, with a deep wound in his neck. You will notice,' said the Sicilian, 'that in this I departed from the general supposition that he had been drowned in the sea, as I had cause to hope that the very unexpectedness of this turn of events would itself in no small way increase the plausibility of the vision; just as, conversely, nothing seemed more dangerous than a too conscientious adherence to nature.'

'I think this was quite rightly judged,' said the Prince, turning to us. 'When it comes to extraordinary appearances, it seems to me that only the more *probable* among them strike us as problematic. If it is easy to understand their revelations, this merely leads to the means by which these are imparted being undervalued; if it is easy to invent these disclosures, the means can easily seem suspicious; for why bother a ghost if you're not going to find out from him something more than what could have been discovered by the aid of mere ordinary reason? But the surprising novelty and difficulty of the revelation is in this case simultaneously a guarantee of the marvellous means through which it has been produced – for who will cast doubt on the supernatural status of an operation when what it has achieved could not have been achieved by natural powers? – I interrupted you,' added the Prince. 'Bring your story to an end.'

The Sicilian continued, 'I let the question be put to the ghost whether there was nothing more that he called his *own* in this world and whether he had not left behind anything that was dear to him? The ghost shook his head three times and stretched one of his hands heavenwards. Before he went away, he pulled from his finger a ring that was found lying on the floor after his disappearance. When the Countess looked more closely at it, she found it was her engagement ring.'

'Her engagement ring!' cried the Prince in astonishment. 'Her engagement ring! But how did you get hold of that?'

'I – it wasn't the real one, my lord – I got it… It was just a counterfeit –'

'A counterfeit!' repeated the Prince. 'To copy it, you needed the real one, and how did you get that since the deceased certainly never removed it from his finger?'

'That is indeed true,' said the Sicilian, not without showing signs of confusion – 'but based on a description of the real engagement ring that someone had given me –'

'That *who* gave you?'

'A long time ago,' said the Sicilian. 'It was a perfectly simple golden ring with the name of the young Countess, I believe. – But you have made me lose my thread –'

'How did things go after that?' asked the Prince with a very dissatisfied and ambivalent expression in his face.

'Now everyone felt convinced that Jeronymo was no longer alive. From this day on, the family made his death public knowledge and went into official mourning for him. The business with the ring left even Antonia with no further doubt, and gave greater force to the Chevalier's wooings. But the violent impression made on her by this apparition plunged her into a dangerous illness which would soon have rendered her lover's hopes forever vain. When she had been restored to health, she insisted on taking the veil, an aim from which she was only to be dissuaded by the most emphatic remonstrances of her confessor, in whom she placed an unlimited trust. Finally, the united endeavours of this man and the family succeeded in forcibly dragging her word of consent from her. The last day of mourning was to be the happy day that the old Marchese intended to make even more of a celebration by the transfer of all his wealth to the rightful heir.

'This day finally came, and Lorenzo was waiting to receive his trembling bride at the altar. Evening fell, and a splendid meal awaited the merry guests in the brilliantly illuminated wedding hall, and joyful music accompanied the boisterous rejoicing. The happy old man had wanted the whole world to share his merriment; all entrances to the palace were thrown open, and anyone was welcome who praised his good fortune. Now among this throng –'

The Sicilian paused, and a shudder of expectation made us hold our breath –

'So, among this throng,' he continued, 'the man I was sitting next to pointed out to me a Franciscan monk, standing as still as a stone pillar, tall and gaunt of stature and ashen-pale in countenance, fixing a sad and serious gaze on the bridal pair. The joy that beamed in every face all around seemed not to have touched this one man; his expression remained immovably the same, like that of a statue among living figures. The extraordinary quality of this sight, which, surprising me as it did in the midst of pleasure, and standing out in such sharp contrast with everything surrounding me at that moment, affected me all the more deeply, leaving such an indelible impression in my soul that through this fact alone I was able to recognise the features of this monk in the physiognomy of the *Russian* (for you will already have realised that he was one and the same person as both this man and your *Armenian*), something which otherwise would have been absolutely impossible. I tried repeatedly to drag my eyes away from that dreadful apparition, but they kept falling back on him against my will, and each time found him unaltered. I nudged my neighbour, and he nudged his; the same curiosity, the same astonishment ran down the whole table, the conversation faltered, there was a sudden general silence; the monk paid it no heed. He stood motionless and unchanged, fixing a sad and serious gaze on the bridal pair. Everyone present was horrified by this apparition; the young Countess alone found a reflection of her own sorrow in the face of this stranger, and gazed with quiet ecstasy on the only person in the whole assembly who seemed to understand and share her grief. Gradually the throng dispersed; it was past midnight, the music started to become softer and more forlorn, the candles to burn lower, eventually casting no more than isolated flickers, the conversation faded to an ever-quieter whisper – and it became more and more deserted in the dimly illuminated wedding hall. The monk stood motionless and unchanged, fixing a sad and serious gaze on the bridal pair.

'The guests rose from the table and dispersed, the family drew into a more narrow circle; the monk remained standing, uninvited, near this narrow circle. I do not know how it came about that nobody was willing to speak to him; but nobody did. The trembling bride was already surrounded by a crowd of her female acquaintances; she sent a pleading, imploring glance to the venerable stranger; he did not return it.

'The men gathered in a similar fashion around the bridegroom. – There was a forced, expectant silence. "– To think we are all so happily enjoying each other's company," finally began the old man, who alone among all of us seemed not to notice the stranger, or was quite unsurprised at his presence, "and my son Jeronymo cannot be here!"

' "So you invited him, and he has failed to come?" asked the monk. It was the first time that he had opened his mouth. We looked at him in fear and amazement.

' "Ah! He has gone to a place from which he will never come," replied the old man. "Venerable sir, you have not understood me. My son Jeronymo is dead."

' "Perhaps he is merely afraid to appear in such company," continued the monk. "Who knows how things stand with your son Jeronymo! – Let him hear the voice that he heard the last! Ask your son Lorenzo to call him."

' "What is the meaning of all this?" murmured everyone. Lorenzo changed colour. I cannot deny that my hair began to stand on end.

'Meanwhile, the monk had stepped over to the drinks table, where he picked up a full glass of wine and set it to his lips. "To the memory of our dear Jeronymo!" he cried. "Whoever loved the departed, let him do the same as me."

' "Wherever you may be from, venerable sir," the Marchese finally exclaimed, "you have mentioned a name dear to us all. I bid you welcome! Come, my friends!" – here he turned round to us and bade the glasses circulate again – "don't let a stranger put us to shame! – To the memory of my son Jeronymo!"

'Never, I believe, was a health drunk in a less hearty fashion.

' "There is still a full glass there. – Why is my son Lorenzo hesitant to drink this friendly toast?"

'Trembling, Lorenzo took the glass from the Franciscan's hand – trembling he brought it to his mouth. "To my much-loved brother Jeronymo!" he stammered, and with a shudder he set it down again.

' "That is the voice of my murderer," cried a fearful apparition that suddenly stood in our midst, its clothes dripping with blood and disfigured by gruesome wounds.

'But do not ask me any more about it,' said the Sicilian, with every sign of dread in his face. 'My senses had left me from the minute I set eyes on the apparition, and the same was true of everyone who was there. When we all recovered, Lorenzo was writhing in the throes of death; the monk and the apparition had disappeared. The Chevalier, wracked by terrible convulsions, was carried off to bed; nobody was at the dying man's side apart from the priest and the pitiful old man who, a few weeks later, followed him in death. His confession lies buried in the breast of the priest who heard his last act of penance, and no living man has ever learnt what it was.

'Not long after this event, it so happened that it became necessary to clear out a well in the rear court of the country estate that had been overgrown by a wild thicket and covered for many years; when the rubble was pulled away, they discovered a skeleton. The house where this happened is no longer standing; the del M**nte family has died out, and in a convent not far from Salerno you can see Antonia's grave.

'So now you see,' continued the Sicilian, when he saw that we were all still overcome by silent consternation and that no one wanted to speak. 'Now you know the origin of my acquaintance with that Russian officer, or that Armenian. Judge now whether I had good cause to tremble before a being who crossed my path in such a terrible manner on two different occasions.'

'Just answer one more question for me,' said the Prince, rising to his feet. 'Have you in your story reported everything concerning the Chevalier perfectly truthfully?'

'As far as I know,' replied the Sicilian.

'So you really always considered him to be an upright man?'

'Yes I did, by God, I did,' came the reply.

'Even when he gave you that ring you mentioned?'

'What? – He gave me no ring. – I never said that *he* gave me the ring.'

'Good,' said the Prince, ringing the bell and making ready to depart. 'And you consider that the ghost of the Marquis de Lanoy,' he asked, returning one last time, 'the one the Russian introduced after your ghost yesterday, really and truly is a ghost?'

'I can't see how he could be anything else,' came the reply.

'Come,' said the Prince to us. The gaoler came in. 'We are ready,' the Prince told him. 'You, sir,' he said, turning to the Sicilian, 'will be hearing more from me.'

'The last question you put to the impostor, my lord, is one I would like to ask you myself,' I said to the Prince, when we were alone again. 'Do you consider this second ghost to be the true and authentic one?'

'I? No, to tell you the truth, I don't, not any more.'

'Not any more? So you *did* believe it?'

'I don't deny that I allowed myself to go along for a moment with the idea that this illusion was something more.'

'And I would like to see the man,' I cried, 'who in these circumstances can *avoid* such a supposition. But what grounds do you now have for retracting that opinion? After what we have just been told about that Armenian, the belief in his marvellous magical power should have increased rather than decreased.'

'Believe what some villain told us about him?' the Prince earnestly interrupted me. 'For I hope you don't still doubt that the man we have been dealing with is a villain?'

'No,' I said. 'But should his testimony for that reason –'

'The testimony of a villain – even if I had no further grounds for casting doubt on it – is of no account when truth and common sense are against it. Does a man who has deceived me several times, who has made deception his business, deserve to be given a hearing in a case where even the most sincere love of truth must prove its immunity to suspicion if it is to win our belief? Does such a man, who perhaps has never spoken a single word of truth for its own sake, deserve to be believed when he bears witness against human reason and the eternal order of Nature? That is the same as saying that I ought to accept the accusations of some notorious criminal when they are levelled against a spotless and blameless innocent person.'

'But what grounds could he have to give such an outstanding testimonial to a man he has so many grounds to hate, or at least to fear?'

'If I don't yet understand those grounds, does that mean he doesn't have any? Do I know in whose pay he was when he deceived me? I admit that I can't yet see through the whole web of his deception, but he has done the cause he is serving no good at all by unmasking himself as an impostor – and perhaps as something even worse.'

'I agree that the business with the ring strikes me as rather suspicious.'

'It's more than that,' said the Prince, 'it is decisive. The moment he received this ring (let me assume for the time being that it all really happened as he said), he must have been certain it was from the murderer. Who other than the murderer could have taken from the deceased a ring that the latter certainly never left off his finger? Throughout his story he tried to persuade us that he himself had been deceived by the Chevalier, while under the illusion that he, the Sicilian, was in fact deceiving *him*. What was this subterfuge meant to achieve if he didn't in his inmost heart feel how much he stood to lose if he admitted he was in league with the murderer? His whole story is obviously nothing but a series of inventions concocted to string together the few true facts that he thought it good to divulge to us. And when I have caught a villain out in ten lies, should I hesitate to find him guilty of an eleventh, or am I supposed to imagine that the fundamental order of Nature, which I have never found to strike a discordant note, has gone awry?'

'I have no answer to that,' I said. 'But the apparition we saw yesterday still remains no less a mystery to me.'

'To me too,' retorted the Prince, 'even though I am tempted to find a key to the riddle.'

'How?' I said.

'Don't you remember that the second apparition, as soon as it appeared, went up to the altar, grasped the crucifix and stepped onto the carpet?'

'That is how it seemed to me, yes.'

'And the crucifix, the Sicilian tells us, was a conductor. So you can see that the apparition was in a hurry to make itself electric. The blow that Lord Seymour aimed at it with his sword was thus deprived of its effect only because the electric shock paralysed his arm.'

'That might be true in the case of the sword. But what about the bullet the Sicilian fired at it and which we heard slowly rolling over the altar?'

'Do you know for certain that it really was the bullet that had been fired that we heard rolling across it? – I will leave aside the possibility that the puppet or the man who was playing the part of the ghost might have been so well armoured that he was proof against bullets and swords. – But think a bit more about *who* it was who loaded the pistols.'

'It's true,' I said, and it suddenly dawned on me. 'The Russian had loaded them. But this happened right in front of our eyes, so how could any deception have occurred?'

'And why might it not have occurred? Did you at that time have any feelings of mistrust towards him that would have made you think it necessary to keep a close eye on him? Did you examine the bullet before he placed it in the barrel of the pistol? It could just as well have been made of mercury or even just of painted clay. Did you pay any attention as to whether he really loaded it in the barrel, or didn't maybe slyly let it drop into his hand? What convinces you – even if he had really loaded them with live ammunition – that he didn't take precisely the loaded pistols into the other pavilion with him, and then substitute another brace of pistols, which he could have done all the more easily as it occurred to no one to observe him, and we were in any case preoccupied with undressing? And might not the apparition, in the very moment the gun-smoke hid it from us, have dropped another bullet, which it had with it for this very purpose, onto the altar? Which of all these possibilities can be ruled out?'

'You are right. But this striking resemblance between the apparition and your dead friend. – I saw him many times at your house, after all, and in the ghost I recognised him straight away.'

'So did I – and the only thing I can say is that the illusion was consummate. But if this Sicilian was able after a few stolen glances at my snuffbox to produce in his painting a fleeting resemblance that managed to take both you and me in, why should the Russian not be even more able to do so? After all, he had free access to my snuffbox throughout the meal, and enjoyed the advantage of remaining totally unobserved from beginning to end; and as I had furthermore confidentially disclosed to him who was portrayed in the picture on the snuffbox… Add to that, as the Sicilian noted, that the characteristic aspects of the Marquis lie precisely in the features of his face that can be imitated without much sophistication – what is still so inexplicable about the whole apparition?'

'But what about the meaning of his words? The information he gave about your friend?'

'What? Didn't the Sicilian tell us that he had cobbled together a similar story out of the few details he had got from me? Doesn't this prove how natural it was that he should fall on just this invention? In addition, the ghost's answers sounded so oracular and obscure that he didn't run any risk of being caught out in a contradiction. If you assume that the impostor's accomplice, the one playing the part of the ghost, was astute and level-headed and knew even a little about the situation – to what lengths could this deception not have been taken?'

'But consider, my lord, how extensive the preparations for such a complex deception must have been on the part of the Armenian! How much time he would have required for it! How much time just to paint the one human face so it would resemble another so faithfully, as you are here supposing! How much time to instruct this pretended ghost, if he were to be insured against committing a gross error! How much attention the little trivial, secondary matters must have required? They had to be dealt with as they might either help the illusion along or else ruin it. And then you must take into consideration the fact that the Russian was absent for no more than half an hour. Could everything, even the absolutely indispensable arrangements, really be managed in no more than half an hour? – Truly, my lord, not even a dramatist, finding himself embarrassed by the implacable three unities of his Aristotle, would have tried to cram so much plot into the interval between acts, or expected his audience to be so completely gullible.'

'What? So you consider it absolutely impossible that all these preparations could have been made in this short half hour?'

'Indeed,' I cried, 'as good as impossible.'

'I can't understand such a view. Does it contradict all the laws of time, space, and physical causality that such a clever fellow as this Armenian incontrovertibly is, with the help of his perhaps equally skilful accomplices, under cover of night, observed by no one, provided with all the tools he required – tools which a man of his trade makes sure he always has with him – that such a man, favoured by such circumstances, could in such a short time achieve so much? Is it completely unthinkable and absurd to believe that with the help of a few words, commands or gestures he could give his accomplices extensive instructions, and without wasting any words he could direct extensive and complex operations? – And surely the only thing that can be allowed to prevail against the eternal laws of Nature is something clearly incompatible with them? So do you prefer to believe in a miracle rather than grant the truth of something that seems implausible? Do you prefer to overturn the powers of Nature rather than believe in the possibility of an artificial and unusual combination of these powers?'

'Even though the matter does not justify such a bold conclusion, you must still confess that it goes far beyond our conceptions.'

'I am almost tempted to dispute even this,' said the Prince, with roguish merriment. 'Why, dear Count – what if it turned out, for example, that people had been working for this Armenian not only during and after that half hour, not just hastily and incidentally, but throughout the whole evening and the whole night? Bear in mind that the Sicilian needed almost three whole hours for his preparations.'

'The Sicilian, my lord!'

'And how can you prove to me that the Sicilian was not just as involved with the second ghost as with the first?'

'What, my lord?'

'That he wasn't the foremost accomplice of the Armenian – in short – that the two of them weren't hand in glove with one another?'

'That could be difficult to prove,' I cried, in no little astonishment.

'Not so difficult, dear Count, as you might suppose. What? Could it be a mere coincidence that these two men met to perpetrate such an unusual and complicated plot against the same person, at the same time and in the same place, that such a striking harmony should have reigned on each side between their operations, and such a well thought-out complicity, that each one should have simultaneously played into the hands of the other? Let's assume that he used the cruder deception to make the more subtle one seem more believable. Let's assume that he tried out the former first to discover the degree of credulity he could reckon on in me; to spy out the ways he could gain access to my trust; to familiarise himself with his subject through this experiment, which could fail without prejudice to his other plan; in short, to try out his instrument. Let's assume that he did this precisely so he could deliberately arouse my attention and vigilance to one matter, thereby diverting it from another more important to him. Let's assume that he had certain items of information to gather, which he hoped would be ascribed to the sorcerer so as to throw our suspicions off the right scent.'

'How do you mean?'

'Let's assume that he bribed one of my servants so as to find out certain secret details – perhaps even documents – that would serve his purpose. I am missing my footman. What prevents me from thinking that the Armenian is involved in this man's disappearance? But chance may so ordain it that I catch on to these tricks; a letter might be intercepted, a servant might talk. His whole reputation is ruined if I discover the sources of his omniscience. So he lays on this sorcerer, who must have some design or other on me. He doesn't neglect to give me an early hint of the existence and intentions of this man. So whatever I might discover, my suspicion will fall on none other than this impostor; and the Sicilian will give his name to the investigations that benefit *him*, the Armenian. This was the puppet with which he had me duped, whilst he himself, unobserved and unsuspected, bound me in invisible ropes.'

'All well and good! But how is it consistent with these intentions that he should help to destroy the illusion and give away the secrets of his art to the eyes of the profane? Surely he must have been afraid that when you discovered the groundless nature of a deception that had been made to seem as plausible as the Sicilian's operation indubitably was, your credulity would be lessened, and this would make it difficult for him to carry out his future plans?'

'What kind of secrets was he giving away to me? You can be sure they were none of those which he intends to use against me. So he did not lose anything by betraying his secrets. – But think how much, on the contrary, he gained when this supposed triumph over deceit and sorcery made me feel safe and secure, when it meant that he could lure my vigilance in another quite opposite direction, and fix my suspicion, still casting about uncertainly, on objects as far removed as possible from the real place of attack. – He could count on the fact that, sooner or later, either impelled by my own mistrust or the urgings of another, I would seek the key to his marvels in the sorcerer's art. – What better could he do than juxtapose the two, thereby handing me the means of comparing them and, by imposing an artificial limit on the latter, heightening or confusing all the more my ideas about the former? How many suppositions did he preclude at one blow through this contrivance! How many explanations that might subsequently have occurred to me did he refute in advance!'

'But the least one can say is that he acted greatly against his own interests when he sharpened the eyes of the people he wanted to deceive and even weakened their belief in his magical power by unmasking his artificial deception. You yourself, my lord, are the best refutation of his plan, if indeed he ever had one.'

'Perhaps he made a mistake in my case – but he was no less sharp a judge in other respects. Could he foresee that precisely the thing that might turn out to be the key to the magic would stick in my memory? Was it part of his plan that the accomplice he made use of would turn out to be so unskilled? Do we know whether this Sicilian did not far exceed the full extent of his powers? – With the ring it is certain. – And yet it is mainly this sole circumstance that aroused my mistrust of the man. How easily a sophisticated and cunning plan can be marred by too coarse an instrument! It was certainly not his idea that the sorcerer should trumpet his fame in the tones of a mountebank – that he should impose on us fairy tales that a moment's thought can see through. An example: how could this impostor have the barefaced cheek to pretend that his wonder-worker must cease all converse with others on the stroke of midnight? Didn't we ourselves see him in our midst at this time?'

'That is true,' I cried. 'He must have forgotten that!'

'But it is part of the character of these people that they take things too far and by overstepping the mark spoil everything, when a more modest and calculated deception would have succeeded admirably.'

'In spite of all that, I still cannot persuade myself, my lord, that this whole affair was no more than a set-up job. What? The Sicilian's terror, his convulsions, his fainting fit, the man's whole pitiful condition that made us feel sorry for him ourselves – is all this supposed to have been just a role he had learnt? Admittedly, theatrical make-believe can be taken so far, but an actor's art has no power to influence his bodily organs to such an extent.'

'As far as that goes, my friend – I have seen Garrick's Richard the Third. And at that instant, were we sufficiently calm, cool and collected to remain uninvolved observers? Could we judge of that man's emotions when we were overwhelmed by our own? Furthermore, the moment of truth is itself, even in the case of a deception, such a crucial occasion for the deceiver, that in *him*, anxious *expectation* can easily produce such powerful symptoms as *surprise* can in the *deceived*. Add to that the sudden appearance of the officers of the law –'

'Indeed, my lord, these men – it's a good thing you reminded me of them. – Would he have dared to expose such a dangerous plan to the eyes of justice? Would he have put the loyalty of his accomplice to such a serious test? – And to what end?'

'That's a matter for *him* – he doubtless knows the kind of men he employs. Do we know what secret crimes may ensure that his man will keep quiet? – You have heard what professional disguise he adopted in Venice. And even if this pretence belongs among the other fairy tales, it surely won't cost him much to save a fellow whose guilt he is the only one to know?'

(And indeed, subsequent events justified all too well the Prince's suspicion. When we asked after our prisoner, a few days later, we received the news that he had disappeared.)

'And to what end, you ask? How else, other than by these violent means, could he drag out of the Sicilian such an improbable and humiliating confession on which his plan so essentially depended? Who but a desperate man who has nothing else to lose will be capable of deciding to proffer such humiliating information about himself? In what other circumstances would we have believed it of him?'

'I grant you all that, my lord,' I finally said. 'Both apparitions must have been tricks; the Sicilian, if you like, simply duped us with a fairy story that his master made him learn; both must have been working with *one* aim in view, in league with one another, and this complicity must be the explanation for all those marvellous coincidences that so amazed us in the course of these events. That prophecy in St Mark's Square, the first miracle, the one that opened the door to all the rest, nonetheless remains unexplained; and what use is the key to all the others when we are in doubt about the solution to this single one?'

'You need to look at it the other way round, my dear Count,' came the Prince's answer. 'You ought to say: what do all those miracles prove when I can demonstrate that beneath them all there was just one single juggler's trick? That prophecy, I confess, goes beyond my powers of understanding. If it were the *only* thing, if the Armenian had concluded his role with it rather than beginning with it – I confess, I don't know how much further it might have led me. In this vulgar company, it strikes me as just a little bit suspicious.'

'Agreed, my lord! But it still remains incomprehensible, and I challenge all our philosophers to explain it to me.'

'But is it really so inexplicable?' continued the Prince, after mulling it over for a few moments. 'I am far from making any claim to the name of a philosopher; and yet I could feel tempted to seek a natural key even for this miracle, or rather to strip it of any appearance of the out-of-the-ordinary.'

'If you can do *that*, my lord,' I retorted with a very sceptical smile, 'then *you* must be the only miracle I believe in.'

'And as a proof,' he continued, 'of how little we are justified in taking refuge in supernatural powers, I will show you two different solutions, which will allow us perhaps to explain these events without doing violence to Nature.'

'Two solutions at once! Indeed, you are really rousing my curiosity.'

'You have read with me the detailed news of the illness of my late cousin. It was in the middle of an attack of malarial ague that he was killed by a stroke. The unusual nature of this death, I confess, impelled me to seek the opinion of several doctors, and what I learnt on this occasion put me on the scent of this piece of sorcery. The deceased's illness, one of the rarest and most dreadful, has these peculiar symptoms: during the ague, it plunges the sick man into a deep sleep from which he cannot be awoken, and which usually, when the paroxysm returns for the second time, kills him in a fit of apoplexy. As these paroxysms return with the strictest regularity, always at a fixed hour, the doctor is, from the very moment at which he has made his diagnosis of the nature of the illness, in a position to indicate the hour of death. The third paroxysm of a three-day attack of ague, however, falls – as is well-known – in the fifth day of the illness, and that is just the length of time needed for a letter to reach Venice from ** where my cousin died. Let us now assume that our Armenian had a watchful correspondent among the deceased's retinue, that he was vitally interested in receiving news from there, that he had the intention of encouraging me to believe in miracles, and the appearance of supernatural powers – and there you have a natural explanation for that prophecy that seems so incomprehensible to you. It's enough for you to derive from it the possibility of how a third party could give me news of a death that was happening at the very moment he announced it, forty miles away.'

'Indeed, Prince, you are here linking together things that, taken separately, may seem perfectly natural, but can only be linked in this way by something no better than magic.'

'What? So you are less astounded by the miraculous than by something *contrived* and merely unusual? As soon as we concede the Armenian had an important plan that was either intended for me or used me as a means to an end – and are we not *compelled* to do so, whatever our opinion of him personally may be? – there is nothing unnatural, nothing forced, in his choice of the shortest way to achieve his purpose. But is there any quicker way of making sure of a man than the powers of persuasion of a wonder-worker? Who can resist a man to whom ghosts are subject? But I grant you, my supposition is feigned; I admit I am not myself satisfied by it. I won't insist on it since I don't consider it worthwhile to call on the help of an artificial and contrived design when mere coincidence is quite enough.'

'What?' I interrupted, 'mere coincidence is enough –'

'Scarcely any more!' the Prince continued. 'The Armenian knew of the danger my cousin was in. He met us in St Mark's Square. The occasion was an invitation to wager a prophecy that, if it turned out false, was merely a waste of breath – and if it proved correct, could have the most important consequences. Success favoured this attempt, and now for the first time he could use the coincidence he was favoured with to put together a coherent plan. Time will clear up this secret or not – but believe you me, my friend,' he said, laying his hand on mine and assuming a very serious expression, 'a man who has higher powers at his beck and call will not need any deception, or will hold it in contempt.'

So ended a conversation that I have set down here in its entirety, as it demonstrates the resistances that needed to be overcome in the Prince, and as, I hope, it will clear his memory of the reproach that he fell blindly and unthinkingly into the trap that an unprecedently devilish plot had laid for him. Perhaps not everyone – *continues the Count von O*** – will, as I write this, look down on his weakness with mocking laughter, and, in the haughty arrogance of their untried and untempted reason, consider themselves justified in condemning him outright of a dreadful crime; not everyone, I fear, would have withstood this first test so manfully. If we now – even in spite of these events that should have had the happy result of putting him on his guard – see him fall; if we find the treacherous attack on him succeeding, even though his good genius had warned him of it when it was still far off, we will be less inclined to mock his foolishness than be amazed at the extent of the knavish ingenuity that even a well-prepared reason succumbed to. Worldly considerations can have no part in my testimony, for the man who would owe me thanks for it is no more. His terrible destiny is accomplished; his soul has long since purified itself at the throne of truth, before which mine too will long have stood when the world reads these pages; but – may I be forgiven for the tears that involuntarily flow at the memory of my dearest friend – I wrote this for the sake of justice. He was a man of great nobility, and he would certainly have been a worthy occupant of the throne which he allowed himself to be seduced into seeking by crime.

Book Two

Not long after these last events – *the Count von O** continues his story* – I began to notice a significant change in the Prince's character. Up until now, the Prince had avoided any more searching test of his belief and contented himself with refining the rough-and-ready, sensual religious concepts in which he had been brought up by means of the better ideas that had impressed themselves on him later, without examining the foundations of his belief. Religious matters in particular, he admitted to me several times, had always appeared to him like an enchanted castle, into which no one could set foot without a shudder, and it was much better to pass them by with respectful resignation, without exposing oneself to the danger of losing one's way in their labyrinths. And yet a contrary impulse irresistibly drew him to carry out investigations that were linked to these matters.

A bigoted, servile education was the source of this fear; it had imprinted on his delicate brain images of terror from which he was never entirely able to free himself his whole life long. Religious melancholia was a hereditary illness in his family; the education that was given to him and his brothers was calculated to produce this disposition, and the people to whom he was entrusted were chosen from this point of view, and were thus either enthusiasts or hypocrites. Stifling every sign of vitality in the boy by gloomy spiritual oppression was the most reliable means of ensuring that one won the greatest approval from the Prince's parents.

This black, nocturnal atmosphere was characteristic of our Prince's entire youth; joy was banned even from his games. All his ideas about religion had a fearful quality about them, and it was indeed their gruesome and uncouth aspects which first took hold of his lively power of imagination and settled most permanently in it. His God was an image of terror, a punitive being; he worshipped God in servile trembling or blind devotion that stifled all energy and initiative. Religion stood in the way of all the inclinations of his youth and childhood, to which a vigorous body and a robust health gave all the more explosive force; religion was locked in a struggle with all that his young heart subscribed to; he never came to know it as something beneficial, merely as a scourge of his passions. And so there gradually flared up in his heart a subdued resentment against it, which with deferential faith and blind fear in his head and his heart, made for the most bizarre mixture – a revulsion against a master for whom he felt in equal measure abhorrence and reverence.

It is no wonder that he seized on the first opportunity to escape from such a stern yoke – but he escaped it in the way a serf flees from his hard master, still dragging around in the midst of freedom the feeling of his servitude. Therefore – as he had not renounced the faith of his youth by his own calm choice; as he had not waited until he had reached the age of reason to take his leave of it at his leisure; and as he had escaped from it as a fugitive, still in thrall to the rights his master exercises over his person – for all these reasons he still had to return to it, even after the greatest attempts to flee. He had escaped still bound in chains, and so inevitably fell prey to each and every impostor who discovered those chains and could make use of them. That one such impostor appeared will, if the reader has not already guessed as much, be revealed in the course of this story.

The Sicilian's confessions left a deeper impression on his character than the whole business really deserved, and the little triumph that his reason had carried off over that feeble deception had noticeably increased his reliance on his powers of reason. The ease with which he had succeeded in seeing through *this* deception seemed to have taken even him by surprise. In his mind, truth and error had not yet separated out so completely for it not to happen frequently that he confused arguments for the former with those supporting the latter; hence it came about that the blow that demolished his belief in miracles at the same time threatened to topple the whole edifice of his religious belief. In this respect, it was as if he was in the same position as an inexperienced man who has, through his own poor choice, been betrayed in friendship or love, and now allows his belief in these emotions in general to wane because he takes mere accidental qualities to be essential properties that are always characteristic of them. A deception laid bare made even truth seem suspicious to him, as he had unfortunately discovered the truth by fallacious reasoning.

This apparent triumph pleased him all the more, the greater the oppression from which it seemed to have freed him. From this point onwards, there arose in him a suspicious cast of mind that did not spare even the things most worthy of respect.

Several factors contributed to keeping him in this disposition and indeed confirming him in it. The solitude in which he had hitherto lived had now come to an end and had inevitably given way to a life filled with distractions. His rank was now public knowledge. Attentions to which he had to respond, social niceties he had to perform because of his rank, dragged him imperceptibly into the turmoil of the great world. His status as well as his personal qualities opened the doors of the most intellectual circles in Venice; soon he saw himself associating with the most brilliant minds in the Republic, both scholars and statesmen. This forced him to widen the uniform, narrow circle in which his spirit had been hitherto enclosed. He started to become aware of the limitations of his ideas, and to feel the need for a more thorough education. The old-fashioned cast of his mind, however many advantages it brought with it, stood in disadvantageous contrast to the ideas current in society, and his lack of acquaintance with the most widely known things sometimes exposed him to ridicule; and he feared nothing so much as ridicule. The unfavourable prejudice that clung to his land of birth appeared to constitute a challenge for him to refute it in his own person. In addition, there was this idiosyncrasy in his character: he was repelled by any attention paid to him that he felt he had only his status to thank for, and not his personal worth. He especially felt this humiliation in the presence of those people who shone through the brilliance of their mind and thereby triumphed over the condition of their birth through personal merit. To see himself treated differently in such society because he was a prince was always a deep source of shame to him, as he unfortunately believed that merely because of his name, he was excluded from any competition. All this together persuaded him of the necessity of making up for the way he had thus far neglected to educate his mind, so as to catch up with the five years' start enjoyed by society wits whom he lagged so far behind.

With this in mind, he chose the most modern books, and devoted himself to reading them with all the seriousness he habitually gave to everything he undertook. But the unskilful hand that was involved in the choice of these writings ensured that, unfortunately, he always came across the books that neither his reason nor his heart were much improved by. And here, too, his deepest predilection prevailed, drawing him, as always, with an irresistible allure, to everything that one should not even try to understand. Only the things relating to such matters attracted his attention and fixed themselves in his memory; his reason and his heart remained empty, while those other faculties of his brain filled themselves with confused notions. The dazzling style of one book swept his imagination away, while the over-sophisticated subtleties of another tied his reason in knots. Together they easily subdued a mind that was prey to anyone who made a sufficiently audacious impression on it.

A book that he had been continually and passionately reading for over a year had enriched him with absolutely no beneficial ideas, but had filled his head with doubts that, as was inevitable in such a consistent character as his, soon found their way, unhappily, to his heart. To cut a long story short: he had entered this labyrinth as an enthusiast with a deep faith, and he left it as a sceptic and, eventually, as an out-and-out freethinker.

Among the circles into which people had managed to draw him, there was a certain closed society called the Bucentauro which, behind the outward appearance of a noble and rational freedom of thought, fomented the most unrestrained licentiousness of opinions and morals. As it counted many priests among its members, and even boasted the names of several cardinals at its head, the Prince was all the more easily persuaded to join. Certain dangerous truths of reason, he thought, could best be held at bay by such people as were duty bound to moderation by their rank, and who enjoyed the advantage of having heard and examined the other side of the question. The Prince was here forgetting that *libertinage* in the mind and morals of persons of this rank is all the more far-reaching as they have one less curb to hold them back, and are not intimidated by the halo of sanctity that so often dazzles the eyes of the profane. And this was the case with the Bucentauro, most of whose members were, through their execrable philosophy, and through the morals that this guide was bound to instil in them, a disgrace not only to their rank, but to the whole of humanity.

The society had its secret grades, and I am inclined to think, to the Prince's honour, that he was never found worthy of admission into their innermost sanctum. Every man who entered this society had, as long as he remained a member, to lay aside his rank, his nation, his religious affiliation, and in short every conventional distinguishing mark, and place himself in a condition of universal equality. The selection of members was in fact very strict, as only intellectual merits allowed one to join. The society prided itself on its extremely elegant tone and cultivated taste, and it did indeed enjoy a reputation for these things throughout Venice. This, as well as the appearance of equality that reigned in it, irresistibly attracted the Prince. An intelligent set of lively and witty acquaintances, instructive conversation, the best people in the scholarly and political world, all converged on it as if to a common centre, and thus concealed from him for a long time the dangers of this association. The spirit of the institution little by little became visible to him through the mask it wore, and possibly people grew tired of having to be on their guard against him, but at all events it was dangerous to attempt escape, and a false sense of shame, as well as concern for his safety, compelled him to conceal his inner dislike.

But merely by becoming intimate with this class of men and their opinions, even if he was not drawn to imitate them, he lost the pure, attractive simplicity of his character and the delicacy of his moral feelings. His understanding, which was supported by so little in the way of real knowledge, could not without outside help see through the subtle but specious reasoning with which they had here ensnared him, and imperceptibly this dreadful corrosive had undermined everything – or almost everything – on which his sense of morality should have rested. He disregarded the natural safeguards of his eternal happiness for sophisms that, at the critical moment, abandoned him and thereby forced him to catch hold of the first arbitrary opinions that were tossed his way.

Perhaps a friend's helping hand might have succeeded in dragging him back in time from this abyss, but, apart from the fact that I learnt about the inner workings of the Bucentauro only much later, long after the damage had been done, I had (right at the beginning of this period) been called away from Venice on an urgent summons. Even Lord

Seymour, a valuable acquaintance of the Prince, whose cool head resisted every kind of deception and would infallibly have served him as a secure support, left us at this time to return to his homeland. Those in whose hands I left the Prince were indeed honest people but they lacked experience, were extremely limited in their religious views, and had as little insight into the real evil that was threatening as they had credit with the Prince. They could counter his insidious sophisms with nothing but the words of a blind, untested faith, that aroused either his anger or his mockery; he saw through them all too easily, and his superior understanding soon reduced those poor defenders of a rightful cause to silence. The others, who subsequently inveigled their way into his confidence, were much more concerned with plunging him ever deeper into error. When the following year I returned to Venice, how much I found that everything had already changed!

One influence of this new philosophy soon showed itself in the Prince's behaviour. The more he enjoyed his life in Venice and won new friends for himself, the more he started to lose the affection of his old friends. Day after day I liked him less, and we saw each other more rarely: in any case, it was less easy to keep in touch. He was caught up in the current of the great world. His doorstep was never empty when he was at home. One entertainment followed hot on the heels of another, feast followed feast, and merriment followed merriment. He was the belle of the ball, the king and the idol of every circle. Just as, in the previous tranquillity of his narrow life he had imagined life in society to be difficult, to his astonishment he now discovered how easy it was. Everything met him halfway, every word that fell from his lips was judged to be excellent, and when he stayed silent, it was felt as a loss to society. Indeed, this happiness that followed him everywhere, this general success really turned him into something more than he actually was, since it gave him confidence and self-reliance. The heightened opinion that he thereby gained of himself induced him to lend credence to the exaggerated and almost idolatrous homage that was paid to his intelligence – something that without this swollen (albeit to some extent well-founded) self-esteem would inevitably have struck him as suspicious. But now this general acclamation merely reinforced what his self-satisfied pride quietly told him – a tribute that was, he thought, his just desert. He would infallibly have escaped from this trap, if he had been allowed to draw breath, if he had only been granted peace and leisure to compare his own worth with the image that was held before his eyes in such a flattering mirror. But his existence was a perpetual state of intoxication, one long giddy whirl. The higher he had been placed, the more he had to do in order to maintain himself at that height; the ensuing state of permanent exertion slowly sapped his strength; peace and quiet had fled even from his sleep. People had seen through his weaknesses and formed an accurate estimate of the passion that they had kindled within him.

His honest attendants soon had to pay for the fact that their lord and master had become an intellectual. Sincere emotions and venerable truths which his heart had once adhered to with the greatest fervour now started to turn into the objects of his mockery. He took revenge on the truths of religion for the oppression under which their delusive ideas had for so long kept him; but as the voice of his heart, which refused to be silenced, struggled against the giddy ideas in his head, there was more bitterness than humour in his wit. His nature started to change; he became capricious. The most attractive aspect of his character, his modesty, vanished; flatterers had poisoned his noble heart. The delicate indulgence of his way of treating others, that had previously made his attendants quite forget that he was their master, now not infrequently gave way to a commanding and imperious tone of voice that was all the more hurtful in that it was not based on the mere discrepancy of inherited rank, for which one can easily be consoled, and to which he himself paid little heed, but on an offensive presumption of his personal superiority. At home, as he often fell into reflections that had been unable to affect him in the social whirl, his own servants rarely saw him looking anything other than gloomy, surly and unhappy, while in other circles he was the life and soul of the party, even though his merriment was put on. With sympathy and sorrow we saw him treading this dangerous path; but in the tumult he had been thrown into, he could no longer hear the feeble voice of friendship, and was now too euphoric to heed it.

Right at the beginning of this period, an important matter at the Court of my sovereign required my presence, and not even the ardent interests of friendship would allow me to postpone it. An invisible agency, that revealed itself to me only much later, had found the means of throwing my affairs there into confusion, and spreading rumours about me that I had to make haste to refute in person. It was hard for me to take leave of the Prince, but it was all the easier for him. Already for some time the bonds that tied him to me had slackened. But his fate had awoken all my sympathy, so I made the Baron von F** promise me that he would keep in touch by letter, a promise that he most conscientiously kept. So for a long time after this I was not an eye-witness of these events: may I be allowed to introduce the Baron von F** in my stead and fill this gap with excerpts from his letters. In spite of the fact that the way my friend F** sees things is not always the same as mine, I have nonetheless decided not to change anything in his words, from which the reader will without much difficulty discover the truth.

*Baron von F** to Count von O***
Letter One 17TH MAY 17**

Thank you, my dear friend, for having granted me the permission to continue, even in your absence, the close contact with you that during your presence here constituted my highest joy. Here, as you know, there is nobody with whom I would dare to voice my opinion of certain matters – however much you may object, the fact is I find these people hateful. Ever since the Prince has become one of them, and especially since you have been snatched away from us, I have been quite abandoned in the midst of this populous city. Z** is finding it easier, and the beautiful ladies in Venice know how to make him forget the insults that he, like me, has to endure at home. And what should *he* have to grieve over? He sees in the Prince, and requires him to be, nothing more than a master of the kind he can find everywhere – but I! You know how closely I feel the joys and sorrows of our Prince in my heart, and I often have cause to do so. It is sixteen years that I have been living with him, and living for him alone. It was as a nine-year-old boy that I came into his service, and from that time, no fate has separated me from him. I grew into the man I am under his eyes; long contact with him has made me grow closer and closer to him; I have been through all his adventures, great and small, with him. I live in his happiness. Until this unhappy year I saw in him only my friend, my older brother, and lived in his gaze as in cheerful sunshine – no cloud darkened my felicity; and now all of this has to be ruined in this wretched city of Venice!

Since you went away, everything round us has changed. The Prince of **d** arrived here last week with a numerous retinue, and added a new and tumultuous animation to our circle. As he and our Prince are so closely related and now get on pretty well with one another, they are not going to separate during his residence here which, I hear, is to last until the Feast of Ascension. It all started as well as could be; for ten days the Prince had hardly been able to draw breath. The Prince of **d** got off to a boisterous start, and would like to carry on in the same extravagant way, as he is soon to leave us, but the problem is that he has infected the Prince with his wild ways, as the latter was unwilling to be left out, and, given the particular relation that exists between the two houses, felt to some extent responsible for asserting the somewhat insecure standing of his own house here. Moreover, in a few weeks our departure from Venice will also be imminent, which at all events will mean that the Prince will be prevented from continuing to indulge any longer in these inordinate expenses.

The Prince of **d**, they say, is here on the business of the ** Order, and imagines that he is playing an important role in it. That he immediately took advantage of all our Prince's acquaintances you can also well imagine. In particular, he was introduced to the Bucentauro with great pomp, as for some time he has enjoyed playing the wit and freethinker, and will only let himself be styled, in his correspondence that extends to all four corners of the world, the 'Prince philosophe'. I do not know whether you have had the good fortune to meet him. He has a highly promising exterior, piercing eyes, the bearing of a connoisseur, a great show of book-learning, a great deal of acquired naturalness (if I may put it like that), and a princely condescension to human emotions combined with heroic self-confidence and an eloquence that can put everyone else in their place. Who could withhold homage from such brilliant qualities in a Royal Highness?

How our Prince's quiet and conscientious worth will fare when compared to this noisy exhibition of superiority, the rest of the story must show.

Since then, many great changes have come about in our way of life. We have moved into a new, splendid house, opposite the Procuratie Nuove, since it was getting too cramped for the Prince in the 'Moor'. Our retinue has been increased by twelve new faces, pages, Moors, guards, etc. – everything is now on a grand scale. You complained of our expenditure when you were with us – you should see it now!

Our personal relations are just as they were – except that the Prince, who is no longer restrained by your presence, is if possible even more monosyllabic and even frostier towards us, and we have little to do with him except assist with his dressing and undressing. On the pretext that we speak French badly and Italian not at all, he manages to exclude us from most of his social engagements – not that I myself am much offended by this; but I think I can see the real reason behind it: he is ashamed of us – and that hurts me; we have not deserved that of him.

Practically the one and only servant he still employs from among us (since you asked to know all the details) is Biondello, whom, as you know, he took into his service after the disappearance of his footman and now, given his new way of life, has become quite indispensable to him. This man knows everyone and everything in Venice, and can turn everything to account. It is just as if he had a thousand eyes and could set a thousand hands to work. He has managed this with the help of the gondoliers, he says. He comes in tremendously useful for the Prince as he can put a name to all the new faces before the latter comes across them at his social gatherings; and the Prince has always found the private information he gives about them to be correct. In addition he can both speak and write Italian and French excellently, and has thus inveigled his way into becoming the Prince's secretary. But I must relate to you an example of unselfish loyalty that is indeed unusual in a man of his station. Recently, a respected merchant from Rimini sought a hearing with the Prince. The reason was a strange complaint concerning Biondello. The procurator, his former master, who must have been an odd fellow, had lived in a state of irreconcilable enmity with his relations, an enmity he wished, if possible, to survive his death.

Biondello had his entire and exclusive trust, and he was in the habit of confiding all his secrets to him; he was obliged to swear to him on his deathbed that he would keep these secrets sacred and never make use of them to the advantage of his relations; a considerable legacy would reward him for this discretion. When his testament was opened and his papers examined, significant gaps and confusions were found, which only Biondello could clear up. But he obstinately denied that he knew anything, left his very considerable legacy to the heirs, and kept his secrets to himself. Substantial offers were made to him by these relations, but they were all in vain. Finally, to escape their importunities, as they were threatening to prosecute him at law, he came into the Prince's service. This merchant, the chief heir, now turned to the Prince, and made even greater offers than before, if Biondello would change his mind. But even the Prince's attempts at persuasion were in vain. Biondello did indeed confess to the Prince that secrets of that kind had been entrusted to him, and he did not even deny that the deceased had perhaps gone too far in his hatred of his family; 'but,' he added, 'he was my good master and my benefactor, and he died firmly trusting my honesty. I was the only friend he left behind in the whole world – which is all the more reason why I should not betray his sole hope.' At the same time he hinted that these disclosures would not redound greatly to the memory of his deceased friend. Is that not to show great tact and nobility? And you can well imagine that the Prince did not persist in trying to shake such praiseworthy resolution. The rare loyalty that he demonstrated to his deceased master won for him the unbounded trust of his present one.

Take care, my dearest friend. How I yearn to have back the quiet life we were leading when you arrived, and for whose quietness you so pleasantly compensated us! I fear that my good times in Venice are over, and I will be all too glad if the same is not true of the Prince. The element in which he now lives is not one in which he can remain happy for long, if my sixteen years' experience does not deceive me. Farewell.

I could never have guessed that our stay in Venice might still turn out to be of some use! It has saved a man's life and I am reconciled to it.

The Prince was recently being brought back home, late at night, from the Bucentauro, and two servants, one of them Biondello, were accompanying him. I don't know how, but the sedan-chair that had been hastily engaged broke, and the Prince found himself obliged to carry out the rest of his journey on foot. Biondello went on ahead; their route led through several dark and secluded streets, and as it was not far off daybreak the lamps were already burning low or had already gone out. They had been walking along for perhaps a quarter of an hour when Biondello discovered that he had lost his way. The similarity between the bridges had confused him, and instead of crossing into St Mark's Square, they found themselves in the *sestiere* of Castello. It was in one of the most secluded streets and there was not a living soul to be seen; they had to turn round and find their bearings in one of the main streets. They had gone only a few paces when, not far from them in an alley, a cry of murder rang out. The Prince, unarmed as he was, tore the stick from the hand of one of his servants, and with the resolute courage that you know him to possess, made for the direction from which this voice had cried out. There he saw three fearsome fellows just about to strike down a fourth who, together with his companion, was defending himself but weakly; the Prince had appeared in the nick of time to prevent the fatal blow. His cries and those of his servants alarmed the assassins, who in such a remote place had not foreseen they would be surprised, and as a result, after inflicting a few light wounds with their daggers, they left their victim and took flight. Half-fainting, exhausted from his struggles, the wounded man sank into the Prince's arms; his companion told the latter that the man he had saved was the Marchese di Civitella, a nephew of Cardinal A**i. As the Marchese was losing a lot of blood, Biondello hastily did what he could to bind up the wound, and the Prince ensured that he was brought to his uncle's palace, which was right nearby and to which he himself accompanied him. Here he left him in peace, without having disclosed his own identity.

But he was betrayed by a servant who had recognised Biondello. The very next morning, the Cardinal appeared, an old acquaintance from the Bucentauro. His visit lasted an hour; the Cardinal was deeply moved when they emerged, there were tears in his eyes and the Prince too was affected. That very evening, he was allowed to visit the wounded man, who the doctor assured them had the very best prospects of recovery. The cloak in which he had been wrapped up had deflected the blow and blunted its force. Since this occurrence, not a single day has gone by on which the Prince has not visited the Cardinal, or the Cardinal him, and a close friendship has developed between the Prince and the Cardinal's household.

The Cardinal is a venerable sixty year old, majestic in appearance, cheerful, fresh and healthy. He is considered to be one of the richest prelates in all the territories of the Republic. He was still dispensing his immense wealth with the carefree attitude of a young man and, though thrifty and sensible enough, not letting any occasion for worldly pleasures pass him by. This nephew was his only heir, though he was allegedly not always on the best of terms with his uncle. However little the old man was an enemy of pleasure, his nephew's behaviour was enough to exhaust even the greatest degree of tolerance. His freethinking principles and his unrestrained lifestyle, unfortunately exacerbated by all the allurement of vice and all the excitement of sensuality, made all fathers fear him and all husbands curse him. It was asserted that he had drawn even this latest attack on himself through an affair he had started up with the wife of the ambassador of **, not to mention the other bad business he had been involved in, from which the Cardinal's prestige and money had only with the greatest difficulty been able to save him. Apart from this, the Cardinal would have been the most envied man in all Italy, as he possessed everything that can make life desirable. In the shape of this single family problem, fortune revoked all its gifts and embittered his enjoyment of his wealth through his perpetual anxiety about not finding an heir to inherit it.

I learnt all this from Biondello. The Prince has found a real treasure in this man. Every day he makes himself more indispensable, every day we discover a new talent in him. A few days back the Prince had got hot and bothered and was unable to sleep. The night-light was put out, and no amount of ringing of the bell could awaken the valet, who had gone out to see his mistress. So the Prince decided to get up by himself and call one of his servants. He had not gone far when he heard the sound of beautiful music coming to him from afar. He moved as if entranced towards the sound of the music and found Biondello in his room, playing the flute, with his comrades around him. He could not believe his eyes and ears, and ordered him to carry on. With admirable ease, Biondello improvised the same melting adagio with the most ingenious variations and all the refinements of a virtuoso. The Prince who is, as you know, a connoisseur, affirms that he could with confidence perform in the finest orchestra.

'I must let this man go,' he told me the following morning; 'it is not in my power to reward him as he deserves.' Biondello, who had heard these words, stepped up. 'My lord,' he said, 'if you do that, you will rob me of my best reward.'

'You are meant for something better than being a servant,' said my master. 'I must not stand in the way of your happiness.'

'In that case, do not force on me any other happiness, my lord, than the one I have already chosen for myself.'

'And to neglect such a talent – No! I cannot let you.'

'So allow me, my lord, to practise it from time to time in your presence.'

And thereupon arrangements were immediately made to this effect. Biondello was given a room next to his master's bedroom where he could lull him to sleep with music and awaken him from his slumber with music too. The Prince wanted to double his salary, but he declined, suggesting that the Prince instead deposit the extra money he graciously intended to give him, and perhaps allow him to avail himself of it soon, as might well be necessary. So the Prince now expects him to come along shortly with a request to make; and whatever request it might be, it has already been granted. Farewell, dearest friend. I impatiently await news from K**n.

The Marchese di Civitella, who is now completely recovered from his wounds, had himself introduced to the Prince by his uncle the Cardinal, and since that day he has followed him like a shadow. Biondello has not told me the truth about this Marchese, or at least he has greatly exaggerated his failings. He is a very likeable man in appearance, and irresistible when you get to know him. It is not possible to bear him any ill will; I was won over at first sight. Imagine the most enchanting figure of a man, endowed with dignity and grace, a face full of spirit and soulfulness, an open and inviting expression, a most silky tone of voice, the most flowing eloquence, the most youthful bloom combined with all the graces of the finest education. He has none of the contemptuous pride, the solemn stiffness, that strikes us as so unbearable in other *nobili*. Everything about him breathes youthful cheerfulness, benevolence, and warm feelings. His dissipations must have been greatly exaggerated to me, I have never seen a more perfect or more attractive picture of health. If he really is as bad as Biondello tells me, he must be a siren whom no man can resist.

He was immediately very free and open with me. He confessed to me with the most likeable frankness that he was not in his uncle the Cardinal's best books, and had probably deserved it. But, he said, he was earnestly resolved to improve, and the credit for this would be entirely the Prince's. At the same time, he hoped he might be again reconciled with his uncle through the Prince, as the Prince was capable of getting the Cardinal to do anything. He had merely been lacking a friend and guide, and he hoped to win both in the Prince.

The Prince also uses all the rights of a guide over him, and treats him with the vigilance and strictness of a mentor. But this very relationship also gives to the Marchese certain rights over the Prince, which he is well able to use to his advantage. He never leaves his side, he is at all the parties which the Prince attends; for the Bucentauro he is – fortunately for him! – as yet still too young. Everywhere he goes with the Prince, he lures the Prince away from society by subtly keeping him busy and occupying his attention. People say that nobody has been able to bring him under control, and the Prince would deserve to be enshrined in a legend if he managed to achieve this huge task. But I am very much afraid that the tables might be turned and the guide might learn from his pupil – something of which, indeed, there seems to be every prospect.

The Prince of **d** has now left – to our general satisfaction, not excluding that of my master. What I foretold, my dearest O**, has really come to pass. Given such opposed characters and the unavoidable clashes that tend to ensue, this good behaviour could not last for ever. The Prince of **d** had not long been in Venice before there arose a serious schism in the intellectual world that put our Prince in danger of losing half of the admirers he had hitherto gained. For wherever he showed his face, he found this rival in his way, who possessed exactly the right dose of petty cunning and self-satisfied vanity to avail himself of even the smallest advantage the Prince gave him. As he had at his command every little trick which the noble Prince refused to lower himself to use, he could not fail in a short time to bring all the weak-minded characters over to his side and place himself at their head – and his party certainly deserved him as their leader.[†] The most sensible thing would no doubt have been not to try and compete with an opponent of this kind, and a few months earlier this would certainly have been the decision the Prince would have made. But now, he had already been swept too far out in the stream to regain the bank quickly. These trifles had, even if only through the circumstances, acquired a certain importance for him, and even if he had really held them of no account, his pride did not allow him to abandon them at a time when to yield would have been seen less as his own free choice than as an admission of defeat. An unhappy exchange of caustic remarks was an additional factor; and the spirit of rivalry that heated his supporters had also seized on him. And thus, so as to preserve the territory he had won, so as to keep a footing on the

[†] The harsh judgement that the Baron von F** allows himself to pass on an ingenious Prince here and in a few places in his first letter will strike everyone who has the good fortune to be well acquainted with this Prince as exaggerated, and they will attribute it to the biased mind of this youthful judge. – Note of the Count von O**

slippery ground which the world's opinion had allowed him, he decided that he must seize every opportunity to shine and attract admirers, and this could be achieved only through an expenditure worthy of a prince; hence the everlasting feasts and banquets, expensive concerts, costly presents and rich entertainments he laid on. And since this strange frenzy soon spread on both sides to the retinues and servants – who, as you know, are much more punctilious on the article of honour than their masters – he had to come to the aid of his servants' zeal with his own generosity. A long catalogue of disasters ensued, all of them the unavoidable consequence of one single, quite forgivable weakness to which the Prince succumbed in a fateful moment!

We have now got rid of that rival, but the damage he has caused is not easily made good. The Prince's coffers are empty; what he had saved up through years of wise economy is gone; we must make haste to leave Venice if he is not to fall into debt, something that he has hitherto taken the greatest care to avoid. The date of our departure has been fixed, and we are merely awaiting bills of exchange.

None of this expense would have been a problem if my master had gained only a single moment of pleasure from it! But he has never been less happy than he is now! He feels that he is not the man he used to be – he does not recognise himself – he is dissatisfied with himself and plunges into new diversions, so as to escape the consequences of the old. One new acquaintance follows another, dragging him deeper and deeper down. I cannot see how it will all end. We must leave – there is nothing further for us to gain here – we must leave Venice.

But, dearest friend, I still have no word from you! How am I to explain this obstinate silence?

Baron von F** to Count von O**
Letter Four   12TH JUNE

Please receive my thanks, dearest friend, for sending me that token of remembrance that the young B**hl brought from you. But why do you mention letters that I am supposed to have received? I haven't received any letter from you, not a word. What a roundabout route they must have taken! In future, dearest O**, when you honour me with letters, send them via Trent to my master's address.

We finally had to take the step, dearest friend, which we had luckily been so able to avoid up until now. – Our bills of exchange have failed to arrive – failed, for the first time, and in this most urgent need – and we have been placed in the necessity of taking refuge in a usurer, as the Prince is happy to pay handsomely for his secret to be kept. The worst thing about this unpleasant event is that it has delayed our departure.

This turned out to be the occasion of a few words being exchanged between me and the Prince. The whole business had been conducted by Biondello, and the Hebrew was there before I knew the slightest thing about it. To see the Prince brought to this extremity wrung my heart and vividly brought back all my memories of the past and all my fears for the future, with the result that I may admittedly have appeared somewhat sullen and morose once the usurer had left. The Prince, who had been made very irritable by the foregoing scene, was pacing in ill humour up and down in his room, the papers were still lying on the table, and I was standing at the window busying myself with counting the panes of glass in the Procuratie. There was a long silence; finally he broke out.

'My dear von F**!' he began. 'I can't stand gloomy faces around me.'

I said nothing.

'Why won't you reply? – Can't I see that your heart is bursting to pour out your disgust? And I insist that you talk. You will otherwise believe that you are keeping to yourself heaven knows what wise admonitions.'

'If I am gloomy, my lord,' I said, 'it is only because I do not find *you* cheerful.'

'I know,' he continued, 'that you think I am not doing the right thing, that every step I take meets with your disapproval – that… – What does the Count von O** write?'

'The Count von O** hasn't written to me.'

'No? Why try and deny it? You pour out your hearts to each other – you and the Count! I know perfectly well you do. But you can still confess it to me. I don't want to pry into your secrets.'

'The Count von O**,' I said, 'still hasn't replied to even the first of the three letters I have written to him.'

'I've done the wrong thing,' he continued. 'Haven't I?' And, picking up a roll of paper, 'I shouldn't have done this, do you think?'

'I can see perfectly well that it was *necessary*.'

'But I shouldn't have placed myself in a situation where it became necessary?'

I was silent.

'Of course! I should never have ventured to indulge my more ambitious wishes, but stayed content with growing old in exactly the same dull way in which I grew up! Just because I escape for once from the dreary monotony of my life up to now, and start looking around to see if there isn't some other source of enjoyment available to me – because I –'

'If you were experimenting, my lord, then I have nothing more to say – the experiences it will have procured for you would have been cheaply purchased even if they had cost three times as much. I was hurt, I admit, to see that the world's opinion should have decided the question as to *how* you could be happy.'

'How fortunate you are that you can scorn it – the world's opinion! I am its creature, and must be its slave. What else are we but opinion? Everything about us princes is opinion. Opinion is our nurse and teacher in childhood, our lawgiver and mistress in our years of manhood, our crutch in old age. Take away from us what we owe to opinion, and the worst of men from the lowest of classes is better than we are, for his fate has helped him find a philosophy which can console him for his life. A prince who laughs at opinion abolishes himself, just like the priest who denies the existence of a God.'

'And yet, my lord –'

'I know what you're going to say. I can step outside the circle that my birth has traced around me – but can I tear from my memory all the crazy ideas that education and early habit implanted in it and a hundred thousand fools have established more and more firmly there? But every man wants to be entirely the man he is, and our existence consists merely of appearing to be happy. Because we cannot be happy in the way you are, should we not be happy at all? If we are no longer allowed to drink our joys pure from their source, are we not even to resort to some artificial satisfaction and take some poor compensation from the very hand that robbed us in the first place?'

'You used to be able to find *that* compensation in your heart.'

'And what if I can no longer find it there? – Oh, what brought us to this? Why did you have to awaken these memories in me? – What if I *have* taken refuge in this tumult of the senses so as to drown out an inner voice that is the bane of my existence – to appease that inquisitive reason that, like a sharp-edged scythe, sweeps back and forth in my brain and with each new swing of its blade lops off a new branch of my happiness?'

'My dearest Prince!' – He had risen to his feet and was pacing with unusual restlessness across the room.

'When everything ahead of me and behind me sinks to nothing – the past lies behind me in dreary monotony like a kingdom turned to stone – when the future has nothing to offer me – when I see the entire circle of my existence enclosed in the narrow confines of the present – who can blame me if I take this meagre gift of time – the present moment – ardently and insatiably into my arms, like a friend I am seeing for the last time?'

'My lord, you must still surely believe in a more permanent good –'

'Oh, let the cloudy image offer itself in more solid form to me and I will press my feverish arms around it. What joy can it give me to grant my favours to appearances that will be gone tomorrow, just as I will? – Isn't all around me in flight? Everything pushes up and thrusts its neighbour out of the way so that it can hastily drink a drop from the fountain of life and then, still thirsty, creep away. In this very moment when I can rejoice in the possession of my strength, there is already some living thing growing and developing and making ready to thrive on my destruction. Show me something that lasts, and I will become virtuous.'

'But what has repressed the benevolent feelings that were once the joy and the guiding principle of your life? To sow seeds for the future, to serve a higher, eternal order –'

'Future! Eternal order! – If we take away that which man has drawn from his own human breast and wrongly imagined to be the purpose of a deity and the law of Nature, what is left us? – What came before me and what will follow me I see as two black, impenetrable veils hanging down at either extremity of human existence and which no living man has yet drawn aside. Several hundred generations already stand before these veils with their torches, trying to guess what may lie behind. Many see their own shadows, the shapes of their passion, magnified and moving across the veil of futurity, and start in fear and trembling at the sight of their own image. Poets, philosophers and founders of states have painted their own dreams on them, cheerful or gloomy as the sky over their heads was darker or brighter; and distance always deceived them with its prospects. Many impostors too exploit this general curiosity and amaze people's excited imaginations with their strange mummeries. Deep silence reigns behind this veil; nobody who has once gone behind it sends back any answer; all that can be heard is the hollow echo of the question, as if it had merely resounded in a tomb. All must go behind this veil, and with fear and trembling they approach it, uncertain who might be standing behind it waiting to receive them; *quid sit id, quod tantum perituri vident*[8]. Of course there were also unbelievers among them who asserted that this veil was merely deluding mankind, and that the reason nothing had been observed was that there was nothing behind it; but in order to convince them, they themselves were rapidly dispatched behind the veil.'

'It was always a rash conclusion if they had no better grounds for their disbelief than the fact they couldn't see anything.'

'Now look, my friend, I am happy to content myself with not wanting to look behind this veil – and so the wisest course will be for me to wean myself away from all curiosity. But while I draw this impassible circle around me and enclose my entire being in the bounds of the present, this brief instant, that I was in danger of neglecting for idle dreams of conquest, becomes all the more significant. What you call the aim of my existence is now of no interest to me. I can't escape from it, I can't do anything to promote it; but I know and firmly believe that I must fulfil such an aim, and that I am indeed fulfilling it. I am like a messenger who is carrying a sealed letter to the place of its destination. What it contains might well be a matter of indifference to the messenger – he is simply out to earn payment for delivery.'

'Oh, how wretched you leave me standing here!'

'But how far we have let our thoughts stray!' the Prince then cried, as he smilingly looked down at the table on which the rolls of paper lay. 'And yet not so far,' he added, 'since you will perhaps understand my adoption of this new way of life. Not even I could wean myself so quickly from my imagined riches, or prise away the main supports of my morality and happiness from the delightful dream with which everything most alive in me hitherto was so closely bound. I yearned for the frivolity that makes the existence of most of the men around me bearable. Everything which seduced me from myself was welcome to me. Shall I admit it to you? I wanted to *sink*, so as to destroy this source of my suffering by deadening my power to achieve anything.'

At this point we were interrupted by a visit. – On a future occasion I will entertain you with a novel development that you could hardly have expected from a conversation like today's. Farewell.

Baron von F** to Count von O**
Letter Five   1ST JULY

As our departure from Venice is now rapidly approaching, this week was to be devoted to catching up on seeing all the sights – paintings and buildings – that one always postpones until the last minute when staying in any place for a long time. In particular, people had expressed their great admiration for Paolo Veronese's *Marriage Feast at Cana*, that can be seen in a Benedictine monastery on the island of San Giorgio. Don't expect me to give you a description of this extraordinary work of art, that as a whole made a startling but not particularly pleasant impression on me. We would have needed as many hours as we had minutes to grasp a composition with a hundred and twenty figures, and over thirty feet wide. What human eye can encompass such a complex whole, and drink in all the beauty that the artist has lavished on it in *one* glance! It is, indeed, a pity that such a substantial work, that should be shown in all its brilliance in some public place where it can be enjoyed by everybody, has nothing better to do than give satisfaction to a few monks in their refectory. The church of this monastery, too, is no less

82

worth seeing. It is one of the finest in the whole city.

Towards evening we had ourselves rowed over to the Giudecca, to spend a pleasant evening there in its delightful gardens. The company, which was not very numerous, soon dispersed, and Civitella, who throughout the day had been seeking an opportunity to speak to me, drew me into an arbour.

'You are the Prince's friend,' he began, 'and he is accustomed to keep no secrets from you, as I have it on very good authority. As I entered his hotel today, a man came out whose occupation is well known to me – and there were clouds on the Prince's brow when I went in to him.' – I tried to interrupt him. – 'You can't deny it,' he continued, 'I knew that man, I got a close look at him. – Could it be possible? Could it be that the Prince has friends in Venice, friends who owe him everything, flesh and blood, and he has been brought to this – to have recourse to such a creature when his need is so urgent! Tell me honestly, Baron! – Is the Prince in financial difficulties? – It is no use your trying to conceal it from me. What I don't learn from you I can certainly find out from that man, who will betray any secret for a price.'

'My lord Marchese –'

'Forgive me. I must seem intrusive, if I am not to risk being ungrateful. I owe the Prince my life, and, much more than my life, a rational use of my life. Am I supposed to sit back and watch the Prince taking steps that cost him money and are beneath his dignity? It's in my power to spare him all this, and am I supposed to suffer in silence?'

'The Prince is not in difficulties,' I said. 'A few bills of exchange that we were expecting to come to us via Trent have unexpectedly not arrived. Doubtless this is an accident – or maybe people were unsure about his departure and were waiting for further instructions from him. This has now been done, and until then –'

He shook his head. 'Don't misunderstand my intention,' he said. 'Here there can be no question of lessening my indebtedness to the Prince – would all my uncle's riches be enough for that? It's a question of sparing him even one single unpleasant moment. My uncle possesses great wealth, and I can dispose of it just as if it were my own property. A happy chance gives me the only possible opportunity of ensuring the Prince can make use of something it is in my power to grant. I know,' he continued, 'how much delicacy there is in the Prince – but it is mutual – and it would be magnanimous of the Prince if he could grant me this small satisfaction, even if it were only in appearance – to lighten somewhat the burden of obligation that weighs on me.'

He would not give up until I had promised to do all I could; I knew the Prince, and could hold out little hope. Civitella was happy for the Prince to lay down whatever conditions he desired, although he confessed that it would offend him deeply if the Prince were to treat him on the same footing as a stranger.

In the heat of our discussion we had strayed far from the rest of the company and were just on our way back when Z** came towards us.

'I'm looking for the Prince – isn't he here, with you?'

'We were just about to go and find him. We were under the impression he was with the rest of the company –'

'They're still all there, but *he* is nowhere to be found. I have absolutely no idea how he managed to slip away from us.'

At this point Civitella remembered that he might have had the idea of visiting the church next door, to which he had enthusiastically drawn his attention only a short while before. We immediately set off to look for him there. While we were still some way off, we discovered Biondello waiting at the church entrance. As we came up, the Prince emerged somewhat hastily from a side door; his face was glowing, his eyes sought Biondello, and he summoned him across. He seemed to be giving him particularly pressing orders, while continuing to keep his gaze fixed on the door that had remained open. Biondello hurried quickly away from him into the church; the Prince, without registering our presence, pushed his way past us, through the crowd, and hurried back to the gathering, which he reached before us.

It was decided to take supper in an open pavilion in this garden, and with this in view the Marchese had, unbeknownst to us, organised a little concert that was something quite special. In particular, we heard a young woman singer who ravished us all both with her lovely voice and her attractive figure. Nothing seemed to make an impression on the Prince; he spoke little and answered distractedly, his eyes were continually and restlessly turning in the direction from which Biondello must come; he seemed to be in a state of great inner turmoil. Civitella asked whether he had liked the church; he could find nothing to say about it. Someone spoke of several excellent paintings which made this church noteworthy; he had seen no paintings. We could see that our questions were irritating him, and fell silent. One hour followed another, and Biondello had still not come. The Prince's impatience rose to a pitch; he officially ended the meal early and went over to an isolated garden path, where he started pacing up and down by himself. Nobody had any idea of what might have happened to him. I did not dare to ask him what had caused such a strange alteration; it has been a long time since I could indulge in my previous intimacies with him. With all the more impatience I awaited Biondello's return, hoping he would solve this riddle for me.

It was past ten o'clock when he returned. The news he brought the Prince did nothing to make the Prince any more talkative. Looking discontented, he walked over to the gathering, the gondola was summoned, and we were soon on our way back home.

That whole evening I could find no opportunity of speaking to Biondello, so I had to go to bed with my curiosity still unsatisfied. The Prince had dismissed us early, but a myriad thoughts kept going round in my head and kept me awake. For a long time I heard him pacing up and down above my bedroom; finally, sleep overpowered me. Long after midnight, a voice awoke me – a hand felt my face; when I looked up, it was the Prince, who, a lamp in his hand, was standing beside my bed. He could not sleep, he said, and he asked me to help him pass the night more quickly. I made to get dressed – he ordered me to stay put, and sat down at my bedside.

'Something happened to me today,' he began, 'which has left an impression that will never fade from my memory. I went away from you, as you know, into the ** Church, which Civitella had made me curious about, and which had already attracted my gaze from afar. As neither you nor he were with me, I walked the short distance alone; I left Biondello waiting for me at the entrance. The church was completely empty – an eerie, chill darkness surrounded me as I stepped in out of the sultry, dazzling daylight. I found myself alone in the spacious edifice, where there reigned a solemn silence like that of the grave. I placed myself under the middle of the dome and surrendered totally to the fullness of this impression; gradually the great proportions of this majestic building started to emerge more clearly, I lost myself in serious and enraptured contemplation. The evening bell rang above me, its tones echoed softly through the building as they did in my soul. Some altar pieces had attracted my attention from a distance; I stepped closer to take a look at them; without noticing it, I had walked right down the one side of the church to the opposite end. Here you take a few steps past a pillar up into a side chapel, where there stand several smaller altars and statues of saints in niches. As I stepped into the chapel on the right, I heard next to me a low whispering, as if someone was talking softly – I turned in the direction of the sound, and – two steps in front of me I caught sight of the shape of a woman. – No! I cannot depict that shape! – Horror was my first emotion, but it soon gave way to the sweetest amazement.'

'And this shape, my lord – can you know for sure that it was something living, something real, not just a painting, not just a product of your imagination?'

'Hear me out. – It was a lady. – No! Up until that moment I had never really seen the fair sex! – Everything was dark all around, the declining daylight fell into the chapel through a single window, the sun fell full on this apparition. With inexpressible grace – half kneeling, half prostrate – she had thrown herself at the foot of an altar: the most striking, loveliest, most perfect outline, unique and inimitable, the most beautiful profile in the whole of nature. Black was the colour of the dress that fitted tightly to her most charming body and gathered round the prettiest arms and spread around her in wide folds, like a Spanish dress; her long, blond hair, woven into two broad plaits that had come loose under their own weight and fallen forward under her veil, flowed in charming disorder down her back – one hand grasped the crucifix, and sinking slowly down she supported herself on her other. But where can I find the words to describe to you the celestial beauty of her face, in which an angel's soul, as if enthroned, displayed the full extent of its charms? The evening sun played on it, and seemed to surround her light and airy golden hair with an artificial halo. Do you recall the Madonna of our Florentine painter? – Here she was, in person, right down to the irregularities of detail that I found so attractive, so irresistible, in that painting.'

As far as the Madonna referred to by the Prince is concerned, the story goes like this. Shortly after you had left, he made the acquaintance here of a Florentine painter who had been summoned to Venice to paint an altar piece for a church whose name I cannot remember. He had brought three other paintings with him that he had intended for the gallery in the Palazzo Cornaro. The paintings were a Madonna, a Heloise, and a Venus almost completely nude – all three of them of exceptional beauty and so equally fine that it was almost impossible to choose between them. The Prince alone showed not a moment's hesitation; hardly had it been placed before him than the painting of the Madonna drew his entire attention to it; in the two others, he admired the artist's genius, but in this one he forgot both the artist and his art so as to live entirely in the contemplation of his work. He was quite marvellously moved by it; he could hardly tear himself away from this painting. The artist, who, as could be seen, inwardly shared the Prince's judgement, obstinately refused to separate the three pictures, and demanded fifteen hundred sequins for them all. The Prince offered him half this sum for the one picture – but the artist insisted on his conditions, and who knows how things would have turned out had a more resolute buyer not been found. Two hours later, all three pictures had gone; we never saw them again. The Prince now remembered this painting.

'I stood,' he said, 'I stood lost in contemplation of her. She did not notice me, she was not in the slightest disturbed by my inopportune presence, so deeply was she immersed in her devotions. She was praying to her divinity, and I was praying to her – yes, I was praying to her. All these images of saints, these altars, these burning candles had not been able to remind me of the fact; but now, for the first time, I was seized by the sense of being in a shrine. Shall I confess it to you? In this instant I believed with rock-like faith in Him whom she held clasped in her beautiful hand. And I could read in her eyes the answer He gave her. Thanks be to her charming devotion! She made Him real to me – I followed her through all His heavenly realms.

'She stood up, and I instantly recollected myself. With bashful embarrassment I slipped away to one side; the noise I made revealed me to her. The unsuspected closeness of a man could have taken her by surprise, and my boldness might have offended her; neither reaction was visible in the look she gave me. Serenity, inexpressible serenity lay in them, and a kindly smile played on her face. She had come down from her heaven – and I was the first happy creature that presented itself to her benevolence. She was still hovering on the last rung of the ladder of prayer – she had not yet touched the earth.

'In another corner of the chapel there were further signs of life. It was an elderly lady who stood up from a pew right behind me. I had not noticed her until then. She was only a few steps away from me; she had seen all my movements. This disturbed me. – I looked at my feet, and then they swept past me.

'I saw her going down the long aisle. Her beautiful figure walked erect. – What lovely majesty! What nobility in her gait! She was no longer the same being as before – new graces – a completely new appearance. They slowly made their way down the church. I followed at a distance, shyly, uncertain as to whether I should catch up with them – or not. – Would she no longer honour me with her gaze? Had she honoured me with her gaze as she walked past me and I could not raise my eyes to her? – Oh, how all these doubts tormented me!

'They stood still, and I – I could not move a foot from where I was. The elderly lady, her mother or whatever relation she was to her, noticed the dishevelment in her beautiful hair and busied herself with rearranging it, meanwhile handing the parasol over for her to hold. Oh, how much dishevelment I wished to see in that hair, and how much clumsiness in those hands!

'The tidying up was finished, and they moved towards the door. I quickened my steps. – One half of her shape vanished – and then the other – now there was just the shadow of her dress, following in her train. – She had gone. – No, she was coming back. She had dropped a flower, she bent down to pick it up – she looked back once more and – for me? Who else could her eyes be seeking within these dead walls? So I was no longer a perfect stranger to her – I too had been left behind by her, like her flower. – Dear F**, I am ashamed to tell you how childishly I interpreted that gaze that perhaps was not even meant for me!'

As far as this last point was concerned, I felt able to assuage the Prince's anxieties.

'Curious,' the Prince continued, after a deep silence, 'is it possible never to have known something, never to have missed it in its absence – and a few moments later to live in and for that single experience alone? Can a single moment make a man so different from himself? It would be just as impossible for me to return to the joys and wishes of yesterday morning as it would for me to return to the games of childhood, now that I have seen *that* object, now that *her* image dwells here – and I have this living, overpowering feeling within me: from now on you can love nothing other than *her*, and in this world nothing else will ever have any effect on you.'

'Just reflect, my lord, on the excitable state of mind you were in when this apparition took you by surprise, and how many things coincided to raise the pitch of your imagination. You were suddenly transported out of the dazzling brightness of the daylight and the tumult of the streets into this stillness and darkness – quite in thrall to the feelings that, as you yourself admit, the silence and majesty of that place aroused in you – in particular, made more receptive towards beauty through the contemplation of beautiful works of art – at once lonely and alone, as far as you were aware, and now all at once, right nearby, surprised by the figure of a girl, when you were not expecting anyone to be around – a girl of a beauty, as I freely grant you, heightened even more by advantageous lighting, a favourable position, an expression of fervent devotion. What could have been more natural than that your inflamed imagination should concoct an ideal figure, something of celestial perfection?'

'Can one's fantasy bring forth something it has never received from outside? – and in the whole extent of my imagination there is nothing that I could compare to this image. Entire and unaltered, as at the moment I saw it, it remains in my memory; I have nothing but this image – but you could offer me a whole world in exchange!'

'My lord, that is love.'

'So must it inevitably be a mere name that makes me happy? Love! – Do not demean my feelings with a name that a thousand feeble souls misuse! What other man has ever felt what I feel? Such a being has never existed before – how can the name pre-exist the feeling? It is a new, unique feeling, newly arising with this new, unique being, and applicable only to her! – Love! I am in no danger from mere love!'

'You sent Biondello away – no doubt to follow the trail of your unknown lady, and find out about her? What news did he bring back to you?'

'Biondello discovered nothing – next to nothing. He found her still at the church door. An elderly, well-dressed man, who looked more like a local citizen than a servant, appeared to accompany her to the gondola. A number of beggars lined up as she went by, and left her with expressions of great satisfaction on their faces. On this occasion, said Biondello, he saw her hand emerge, and several precious stones glittered on it. She said a few words to her companion that Biondello didn't understand; he told me it was Greek. As they had some way to go to get to the canal, quite a crowd started to gather; the extraordinary sight brought all the passers-by to a halt. Nobody knew her. – But beauty is a natural queen. They all respectfully made way for her. She let down a black veil over her face that covered half her robe, and hurried into the gondola. Biondello kept the vessel in view as it moved down the entire length of the Giudecca canal, but he was prevented from following it any further by the press of people.'

'But he must have had a good enough view of the gondolier for him to be able to recognise him?'

'He ventures to think he could trace the gondolier; but he is not among those he is acquainted with. The beggars he questioned could give him no further information other than that the Signora had been appearing here for a few weeks, always on a Saturday, and always gave them a gold coin to share out among themselves. It was a Dutch ducat, which he changed for them and brought to me.'

'So she is a Greek, and of high standing, it appears, or at least a woman of property, and a giver of charity. That is as far as our surmises can go, my lord – almost too far! But a Greek woman – in a Catholic church?'

'Why not? She might have abandoned her faith. And moreover – there is still something mysterious about it. – Why just once a week? Why only on Saturdays in this church, at a time when it is usually deserted, as Biondello tells me? – We need wait only for next Saturday to find out. But until then, dear friend, help me to leap across this gulf of time! But it's no use! Days and hours go their slow, calm way, and my desire has wings.'

'And when that day finally comes – what then, my lord? What do you suppose will happen then?'

'What will happen? – I will see her. I will ascertain the reason why she is here. I will find out who she is. – Who she is? – What importance can that be to me? What I saw made me happy, so I already know everything that can make me happy!'

'And what about our departure from Venice, which has been fixed for the beginning of next month?'

'How could I have known that Venice would still hold such a treasure for me? – You are asking me about the life I was leading until yesterday. I tell you that I *am*, and wish to *be*, only from today.'

Now I thought I had found the opportunity to keep my promise to the Marchese. I impressed upon the Prince that his further stay in Venice would be impossible, given the depleted state of his coffers, and if he were to extend his stay beyond the agreed date, he would not be able to count on much support from his Court. On this occasion I had learnt what had hitherto been kept from me: he was receiving secret and substantial loans from his sister, the reigning ** of **, without the knowledge of his other brothers, and she was quite prepared to double this amount, if his Court left him in the lurch. This sister, a pious religious enthusiast, as you know, believes that the great economies she makes in her really quite austere Court can be used in no better way than to help out a brother whose wise benevolence she is aware of and whom she honours and reveres. I had indeed known for a long time that there was a close relation between them, and that they frequently exchanged letters; but as the Prince's expenditure had hitherto been adequately financed from the usual sources, I had never guessed at this hidden resource. It is thus clear that the Prince had had expenses that were unknown to me and still are; and I may judge from the other aspects of his character, they are certainly expenses that redound to his honour. And I had imagined I had fathomed him! – After this discovery, I was all the more eager to reveal to him the Marchese's offer – which, greatly to my surprise, was accepted without the slightest difficulty. He gave me full powers to transact this business with the Marchese whatever way I thought best, and then immediately to settle with the usurer. A letter should be sent to his sister without delay.

It was morning when we separated. However disagreeable I find and must find this incident, for more than one reason, the most unpleasant thing about it all is that it threatens to prolong our stay in Venice. From this dawning passion I expect much more good than bad. It is perhaps the most powerful means of dragging the Prince back down from his metaphysical daydreams to ordinary humanity: it will, I hope, lead to the usual crisis and, like an artificial illness, eradicate the natural illness too.

Farewell, dearest friend. I have written all this to you straight after the events it recounts. The post is just about to go; you will receive this letter with the previous one on the *same* day.

*Baron von F** to Count von O***
Letter Six

This Civitella really is the most obliging man in the world. The Prince had only just left me the other day when a note came from the Marchese in which his former offer was repeated to me in the most pressing terms. I immediately sent him a bond for six thousand sequins in the Prince's name; in less than half an hour it came back with twice the sum, in bills of exchange as well as cash. The Prince finally agreed to this increase in the amount, but he insisted that the bond, which was drawn for a period of just six weeks, should be accepted.

This whole week has been taken up in investigations into the mysterious Greek lady. Biondello set all his wheels turning, but up until now without avail. He did manage to find the gondolier, but he could get nothing further from him than that he had set down both ladies on the island of Murano, where two sedan-chairs had been waiting for them, which they got into. He made them out to be English women, since they spoke a foreign language and had paid him in gold. Neither could he identify their companion; he thought he looked like a manufacturer of mirrors from Murano. Now we at least knew that there was no point looking for her in the Giudecca and that in all probability she lived on the island of Murano, but the problem was that the description the Prince gave of her was inadequate for her to be recognised by a third party. The very passionate attentiveness with which he had devoured her with his eyes had, as it were, prevented him from *seeing* her; he had been quite blind to everything that would have principally absorbed the attention of any other man; given his description of her, people would have been tempted to seek her in Ariosto or Tasso rather than on a Venetian island. In addition, the enquiries had to be prosecuted with the greatest precaution, for fear of arousing offence. As Biondello was, apart from the Prince, the only one who had – at least through her veil – seen her and thus would be able to recognise her, he tried to be present in all the places where she might at any time be supposed to be; the poor man's life was, all week long, nothing but a perpetual running too and fro through all the streets in Venice. In particular, no pains were spared to make investigations in the Greek church, but all of them came to nothing, and the Prince, whose impatience increased with every expectation that was dashed, finally had to console himself with the prospect of the following Saturday.

His restlessness was dreadful. Nothing could distract him, nothing could restrain him. His whole being was in a state of feverish agitation, he was averse to all society, and in his solitude the disease grew. But never had he been more besieged by visitors as in precisely this week. His imminent departure was common knowledge, and everyone was thronging to see him. These people had to be kept occupied so as to divert their suspicions away from him; *he* had to be occupied so as to distract his mind. In these trying circumstances, Civitella hit on the idea of gambling, and so as to drive away at least the common hordes, he suggested that the stakes should be set high. At the same time he hoped to awaken in the Prince a temporary liking for gambling that would soon stifle the romantic character his passions had assumed; and that it would always be possible to wean him away from this new distraction. 'Cards,' said Civitella, 'have preserved me from many a folly I was about to commit, and made up for many a folly I had already committed. The peace of mind and the good sense that two lovely eyes had robbed me of were often restored to me at the faro table[9], and women have never had more power over me than when I didn't have enough money to gamble.'

I leave it open to question to what extent Civitella was right – but the remedy we had hit upon soon started to prove even more dangerous than the disease they were supposed to cure. The Prince, who was able to give the game a transient charm only through wagering for high stakes, soon found himself overstepping all bounds. For once, he was quite out of his element. All his actions were filled with passion; everything he did bore the mark of the impatient vehemence that now reigned within him. You know his indifference to money; here it turned into complete insensitivity to its value. Gold coins flowed like drops of water through his fingers. He lost almost uninterruptedly, as he played without the slightest care or attention. He lost huge sums since he played like a desperate gambler. – Dearest O**, my heart shakes as I write it – in four days the twelve thousand sequins, and even more than that, had gone.

Do not reproach me. I blame myself for it quite enough. But could I prevent it? Would the Prince listen to me? Could I do anything other than point out to him the error of his ways? I did what lay in my power. I cannot find myself guilty.

Civitella too lost a considerable amount; I won around six hundred sequins. The Prince's unprecedented ill luck caused a sensation; all the more reason for him not to be able to leave the game. Civitella, whose joy at being able to oblige him was visible, immediately advanced the required sum. The hole was filled, but the Prince owes the Marchese twenty-four thousand sequins. Oh, how I yearn for the savings of his pious sister! – Are all princes like this, dearest friend? The Prince behaves exactly as if he had shown the Marchese a great honour, and the latter – at least plays his part well.

Civitella tried to reassure me by saying that this very excess was the most powerful means of making the Prince see reason again. There was no urgency about the money. He himself was not in the slightest bothered by this hole in his finances and at any moment would be at the Prince's service with three times as much. Even the Cardinal assured me that his nephew had the right idea and that he himself was prepared to stand as a guarantor.

The saddest thing was that these huge sacrifices did not even have the desired effect. You might think that the Prince at least took a lively interest in the game. Nothing could be further from the truth. His thoughts were far away, and the passion that we were trying to repress seemed merely to draw more nourishment from his ill luck in the game. When a decisive moment in play was imminent and everyone crowded with anticipation round his table, his eyes sought Biondello to read in advance any news he might perhaps be bringing with him. But each time, Biondello had nothing to report – and the Prince's hand always lost.

Incidentally, the money he lost fell into very needy hands. A few of their 'Excellencies' who, as malicious rumour reports, have to take their frugal midday meal home from the market themselves in their senatorial caps, entered our house as beggars and left it as men of wealth. Civitella pointed them out to me. 'Look,' he said, 'how many poor devils can profit from the fact that a sensible man takes it into his head to behave oddly! But I like that. It is princely and kingly! A great man must after all make people happy even in his eccentricities, and like a river in flood fructify the fields on either side.'

Civitella's thoughts are all fine and noble – but the Prince owes him twenty-four thousand sequins!

The Saturday so long awaited finally came, and my master could not be restrained from betaking himself to the ** Church directly after midday. He took up his place in the very same chapel where he had seen his unknown lady for the first time, but positioned himself where she would not immediately notice him. Biondello had been given orders to stand guard at the church door and there strike up acquaintance with the lady's companion. I had taken it upon myself to pretend to be an innocent passer-by and take a seat in the same gondola on the way back, so as to follow the unknown woman's trail further, if all else failed. At the same place where they had, according to the gondolier, had themselves set down the previous time, two sedan-chairs were hired; to crown it all, the Prince requested the chamberlain, Z**, to follow in a separate gondola. The Prince himself would live merely for the prospect of seeing her and, if successful, would try his luck in the church. Civitella kept right out of it, since his reputation with the fair sex in Venice was too bad for his involvement not to make the lady mistrustful. You can see, dearest Count, that it would not be for the want of trying if the beautiful stranger escaped us.

Never were more ardent wishes nursed in a church as in this one, and never were they more cruelly disappointed. The Prince waited until after sunset, his expectations aroused by every sound that came near his chapel, every creaking of the church door – seven full hours – and no Greek woman. I will not try to describe his state of mind. You know what a hope deferred is – and a hope on which one has lived almost exclusively for seven days and seven nights.

Baron von F** to Count von O**
Letter Seven   JULY

The Prince's mysterious unknown lady reminded Marchese Civitella of a romantic apparition that had presented itself to him some time ago, and so as to distract the Prince he showed himself willing to share it with us. I will relate it to you in his own words. But the merry and spirited way he has of enlivening everything he says is obviously something I cannot convey.

'Early last year,' Civitella told us, 'I had the misfortune to incur the wrath of the Spanish ambassador who, in his seventieth year, had committed the folly of wanting to take for his wife an eighteen-year-old Roman girl. His vengeance pursued me, and my friends advised me to escape its effects by quickly taking flight, until either the hand of Nature or an amicable settlement had freed me from this dangerous foe. As I found it much too difficult to abandon Venice entirely, I took up residence in a distant quarter of Murano, where I lived in a solitary house under an assumed name, stayed in hiding all day long, and devoted the night to my friends and my pleasures.

'My windows overlooked a garden that on the west was bounded by the wall encircling a monastery, but on the east protruded into the lagoon like a small peninsula. The garden was laid out in the most delightful way, but was rarely visited. It was my custom every morning, after my friends had left me and before I retired to bed, of whiling away a few more minutes at the window, watching the sun rising over the gulf and then bidding it good night. If you have never indulged in this pleasure, my lord, I can recommend this spot to you, the most exquisite, perhaps, in all Venice, if you wish to enjoy this splendid sight. The purple hues of night lie over the deeps, and a golden haze announces the sunrise along the distant rim of the lagoon. Earth and sky tranquilly await the dawn. In two seconds, there it stands, full and perfect, and all the waves are aflame – it is a ravishing spectacle!

'One morning, as I was surrendering to the pleasure of this sight in the usual way, I suddenly noticed that I was not the only spectator of this scene. I thought I could hear voices in the garden, and when I turned to look in the direction from which they came, I spotted a gondola that was landing at the water's edge. A few moments later some people appeared in the garden, walking slowly up and down the path, like people out for a stroll. I could see that it was a man and a woman who had a little black boy with them. The woman was dressed in white, and there was a diamond ring glittering on her finger; the wan dawn light meant I couldn't make out any more.

'My curiosity was aroused. It was certainly a lovers' tryst – but in this place and at such an unusual hour! – for it was hardly three o'clock and everything still lay in the half-light of dawn. The idea struck me as original, one that would suit a novel. I decided to await the end.

'In the covered arbours of the garden I soon lost them from sight, and it was a long time before I saw them again. Meanwhile, a pleasant song filled the neighbourhood. It came from the gondolier who, by doing this, made the time go by more quickly in his gondola, and he was being echoed by a comrade nearby. They sang stanzas from Tasso; time and place matched them harmoniously, and the melody melted sweetly away in the surrounding silence.

'Meanwhile day had broken and details could be made out more clearly. I looked for the people I had seen. Hand in hand they were now going up a broad garden path and often halting, but they had their backs turned to me and they were heading away from my residence. The grace of their movements as they walked led me to deduce that they were of aristocratic standing, and a noble, angelically beautiful stature suggested she was of unusual beauty. They spoke little, it seemed to me, though the lady said more than her companion. They seemed to pay no attention at all to the spectacle of the sunrise that was now in its finest splendour spreading above them.

'As I brought over my little telescope and aimed it in the right direction to bring this strange apparition as close to me as possible, they suddenly disappeared once more into a side path, and a long time elapsed before I caught sight of them again. The sun had now completely risen, they came right up beneath me and looked straight towards me. – What a celestial apparition I saw! – Was it the effect of my imagination, was it the magic of the light? I thought it was a heavenly creature I was seeing, and my eye flinched, smitten by the dazzling light. – So much grace with so much majesty! So much spirit and nobility with so much youthful blossom! – It is no good my trying to describe it to you. I had never seen real beauty before that moment.

'They lingered near me, intent on their conversation, and I had entire leisure to lose myself in that wonderful sight. But hardly had my eyes fallen on her companion than even her beauty was no longer powerful enough to tear them away from him. He struck me as a man in the prime of life, on the slim side and tall and noble in stature – but no human brow had ever bedazzled me with so much intellect, so much loftiness, so much that was divine. I myself, although I was safe from all discovery, was unable to sustain the piercing gaze that darted forth like flashes of lightning from beneath his dark eyebrows. Around his eyes lay a quiet and poignant sadness, and a hint of benevolence around his lips softened the melancholy seriousness that overshadowed his entire face. But there was something in the cast of his features that was not European, and this, together with a type of dress that had been boldly and happily chosen from the most varied kinds of costume, although with quite inimitable taste, gave him a demeanour of strangeness that in no small measure heightened the impression made by his whole being. Something wild in his gaze might have suggested a religious enthusiast, but his gestures and the grace of his outer appearance all betokened a man well versed in the ways of the world.'

Z**, who, as you know, always has to say everything that comes into his head, could no longer restrain himself at this point. 'Our Armenian!'

98

he exclaimed. 'Our Armenian in person, nobody else!'

'What Armenian, if one may ask?' said Civitella.

'Hasn't anybody told you about that farce yet?' said the Prince. 'But no interruptions! I'm starting to get interested in your man. Carry on with your story.'

'There was something incomprehensible in his behaviour. His eyes rested meaningfully and passionately on her when she was looking away, but he looked down when her eyes met his. "Is this man out of his mind?" I thought. I could easily have stayed there for an eternity gazing at nothing else.

'The foliage stole them away from me again. I waited a long, long time to see them reappear, but in vain. I finally spotted them from another window.

'They were standing in front of a pond, some little distance apart, both wrapped in a profound silence. They might have been standing there in that posture for quite some time. Her open, soulful eyes rested questioningly on him and seemed to be reading every burgeoning thought as it appeared on his brow. He, as if not feeling the courage within himself to look at it directly, surreptitiously sought her image in the reflective surface of the water, or stared fixedly at the dolphin that was spouting the water into the basin. Who knows how long this mute play-acting would have lasted if the lady could have endured it? With the most kindly grace the lovely creature went up to him, draped her arm around his neck, took hold of one of his hands and brought it up to her mouth. The cold man calmly allowed her to do this and her embrace was not returned.

'But there was something in this scene that moved me. It was the man who moved me. A vehement emotion seemed to be working in his breast, an irresistible power seemed to draw him to her, and an invisible arm to be pulling him back. This struggle was quiet but painful, and the source of temptation at his side so beautiful. No, I thought, he is attempting too much. He will, he must succumb.

'At a secret signal from him, the little Negro disappeared. I was now awaiting a scene of a sentimental kind, a supplication made on bended knee, a reconciliation sealed with a thousand kisses. None of this happened. The incomprehensible man took from a wallet a sealed packet and handed it to the lady. Sorrow crossed her face when she saw it, and a tear glinted in her eye.

'After a short silence they separated. From a side path there walked up to them an elderly lady who had stayed at a distance the whole time and whom I now noticed for the first time. Slowly they walked away, the two women in conversation with each other, during which time he saw his opportunity to remain unnoticed behind them. Irresolute and staring after them, he stood awhile and moved forward and then halted again. Then he suddenly disappeared into the bushes.

'The ladies ahead finally looked round. They seemed disquieted not to see him any more, and halted, seemingly waiting for him. He did not come. Their eyes wandered anxiously around, they hurried this way and that. My eyes too sought him everywhere in the garden. He wasn't there. He was nowhere.

'Suddenly I heard a swishing noise on the canal, and a gondola pushed off from the bank. It was him, and I had to make an effort not to call out to her. Now everything was clear – it was a scene of separation.

'She seemed to *guess* what I *knew*. Faster than the other woman could follow her she hurried to the canal bank. Too late. The gondola was speeding away as fast as an arrow, and only a white handkerchief could be seen still fluttering in the air far away. Soon afterwards I saw the women too cross the canal.

'When I awoke from a short sleep, I had to laugh at my delusion. My imagination had prolonged these events in a dream, and now the truth too had become dreamlike. A girl, as ravishing as a houri, taking a stroll with her lover before dawn in a secluded garden. A lover who can find nothing better to do at such a time – this struck me as a composition which at best the imagination of a dreaming man could venture to invent and explain. But the dream had been too beautiful for me not to wish to renew it as often as possible, and even the garden had become dearer to me since I had peopled my imagination with such delightful shapes. Several cheerless days that followed that morning kept me from the window, but the first fine evening drew me involuntarily to it. Judge of my astonishment when I looked for and soon saw the gleam of my unknown lady's white dress. She was there, in person. She was real. I hadn't just dreamt it.

'The same matron as before was with her, leading along a small boy, but she herself was wrapped in her own thoughts and walking apart. They visited all the places that had been made memorable by her companion on the previous occasion. She lingered for a particularly long time by the pond, and her eyes, staring fixedly at it, seemed to be seeking the beloved image in vain.

'If that noble beauty had intoxicated me away the first time, today it exercised its effect on me with a force that was gentler albeit, no less strong. I now had perfect freedom to contemplate this heavenly image; the amazement caused by my first sight of her gradually gave way to a sweet emotion. The halo around her vanished, and I saw in her no more than the most beautiful of all women, setting my senses aflame. In this moment my decision was made. She must be mine.

'While I was considering in myself whether to go down and approach her or whether, before daring to do so, I should find out more about her, a little gate in the monastery wall opened, and a Carmelite monk stepped out. Hearing the noise he made, the lady left her place and I saw her walking with quick steps up to him. He took a paper from his breast, which she hastily snatched from him, and a vivacious expression of joy seemed to spread at once over her face.

'In this very moment my usual evening visit brought me away from the window. I took pains to avoid that spot, not wishing to allow anyone else to have a chance of stealing my prey. I had to endure a whole hour in this state of distressing impatience, until I finally succeeded in getting rid of that unwanted visitor. I hurried back to my window, but they had all vanished!

'The garden was quite empty when I went down. There was no vessel in the canal. No trace of any people. I did not know from which district she had come, nor where she had gone to. As I carried on walking, my eyes turning in every direction, something white gleaming on the sand in the distance caught my gaze. When I went up to it, I found it was a paper, folded in the shape of a letter. What else could it be but the letter which the Carmelite had delivered to her? "A happy find!" I exclaimed. "This letter will reveal the whole mysterious situation to me, and make me master of her fate."

'The letter was sealed with a sphinx; it bore no superscription, and was written in code, but this did not deter me, as I can decipher codes. I quickly copied it, for it was to be expected that she would soon realise she had lost it and come back to look for it. If she couldn't find it, this would inevitably demonstrate to her that the garden was visited by more than one person, and this discovery could easily scare her away for good. What worse outcome could there be for my hopes?

'What I had anticipated happened. I had hardly finished my copy when she reappeared with the same lady companion as previously, both of them anxiously searching. I fastened the letter to a slate I had prised away from the roof, and dropped it in a place she would have to pass by. Her delightful expression of joy on finding it rewarded me for my magnanimity. With a penetrating, searching look, as if she wanted to find out which unholy hand had touched it, she examined it thoroughly, turning it over and over, but the satisfied expression with which she put it away proved that she was quite without suspicion. She went off, and a parting glance took a grateful leave of the tutelary gods of the garden who had so loyally guarded the secret of her heart.

'Now I hastened to decipher the letter. I tried several languages; finally, I succeeded with English. Its contents were so remarkable that I memorised them by heart.'

I have been interrupted. I'll conclude the story another time.

Baron von F** to Count von O**
Letter Eight

No, dearest friend. You are doing an injustice to the good Biondello. You are certainly harbouring a false suspicion. I'll grant you may be right about Italians in general, but this one is honest.

You find it strange that a man of such brilliant talents and such exemplary conduct could lower himself to be a servant unless he had secret motives for so doing; and you deduce that these motives must be suspicious. Why? Is there anything so very new about a man of intelligence and merit trying to make himself obliging to a Prince who has the power to make him happy? Is it somehow dishonouring to serve him? Doesn't Biondello show all too clearly that his devotion to the Prince is personal? He has indeed confessed to him that he has his heart set on making a certain request of him. This request will doubtless clear up the whole mystery for us. Secret motives he may well have, but might these not be innocent ones?

It surprises you that this Biondello kept concealed for those first months – precisely the ones during which you were still favouring us with your presence – all the great talents that he has now revealed, and that he in no way drew attention to himself. That is true; but how could he have found an opportunity to distinguish himself at that time? The Prince did not need him yet, and his other talents had to wait for chance to discover them to us.

But he quite recently gave us a proof of his devotion and honesty that will quite demolish all your doubts. The Prince is being observed. They are trying to find out secret details of his way of life, his acquaintances and his relations. I don't know who is curious to learn these facts. But listen.

There is here on San Giorgio a house of ill repute where Biondello is often seen going in and coming out; maybe he has a sweetheart there, I don't know. A few days ago he was there again; he found a number of people gathered, advocates and government officials, jovial friars and friends of his. They were surprised and overjoyed to see him again. Old acquaintances were renewed, each of them told his story up until that moment, and Biondello too entertained them with his. He did it in a few short words. They wished him luck in his new position, they had already heard about the brilliant lifestyle of the Prince of **, in particular his generosity towards people who are able to keep a secret; his links with Cardinal A**i were known to all, as was the fact that he loves gambling, etc. Biondello stopped short. – They joked with him, claiming that he is pretending to be a man of mystery, while they know that he is the chargé d'affaires of the Prince of **; both the advocates made him sit between them, the bottle was soon busily being emptied – he was urged to drink; he excused himself, as he can't tolerate wine, but he did drink so he could pretend to get drunk.

'Yes,' the one advocate finally said, 'Biondello understands his trade, but he still hasn't finished his apprenticeship yet, he's only a novice.'

'What do I still need to learn?' asked Biondello.

'He knows the art,' said another, 'of keeping a secret to himself, but he doesn't yet know the other art, that of being able to divulge it to his advantage.'

'Could a buyer for my secret be found?' asked Biondello.

The other guests at this point left the room, he remained tête-à-tête with the two men who came out with their request. To cut a long story short, I will simply say that he was to provide them with information on the Prince's dealings with the Cardinal and his nephew, give the source from which the Prince drew his money, and intercept for them all the letters that would be written to the Count von O**. Biondello managed to put them off for now, but he could not draw from them the identity of the man who had put them up to it. Given the brilliant offers that were being made to him, he was forced to deduce that the enquiries must stem from a very wealthy man.

Yesterday evening he told my master about the whole business. The Prince at first wanted simply to have the plotters apprehended, but Biondello made objections. They would merely have to be freed subsequently, and then he would have endangered his entire credit among people of that class, and maybe his very life. All those men stuck together, and all stood up for each other; he would rather have the high council in Venice as his enemy than be regarded as a notorious traitor by them; and he would no longer be of any use to the Prince once he had lost the trust of this class of men.

We turned over in our minds who might be behind all this. Who is there in Venice who thinks it important to know my master's income and expenditure, what he does with Cardinal A**i and what he writes to you? Could it be yet another legacy of the Prince of **d**? Or maybe the Armenian is on the move again?

The Prince is dizzy with love and joy. He has his Greek lady back. Hear how it happened.

A stranger who had come via Chiozza and was able to tell us all about the beautiful situation of that town on the gulf made the Prince curious to see it. Yesterday this plan was put in operation and to avoid all constraint and expense, nobody was to accompany him other than Z** and myself, together with Biondello, and my master wished to remain incognito. We found a vessel that was just about to set off for there, and we engaged it. The company was very mixed, but not numerous, and the outward journey was uneventful.

Chiozza is built on wooden piles rammed down, like Venice, and is said to count about forty thousand inhabitants. There are few members of the aristocracy, but at every step you come across fishermen or sailors. Anyone wearing a wig and cloak is considered a rich man; a cap and overcoat are the signs of a poor man. The town is finely situated, but only if you haven't seen Venice.

We did not stay long. The boat's captain, who had several other passengers, had to be back in Venice early, and there was nothing to keep the Prince in Chiozza. Everyone had already taken their place on board ship by the time we arrived. As the company had made itself so irksome on the outward journey, this time we took a room to ourselves. The Prince enquired who else was there. A Dominican, was the reply, and a few ladies who were returning to Venice. My master was not curious to see them, and immediately took to his room.

The Greek lady had been the topic of our conversation on the outward journey, and was so again on the return journey. The Prince passionately evoked her appearance in the church again; plans were devised and rejected; hours went by in minutes; before we had realised it, Venice lay before us. Some of the passengers disembarked, the Dominican among them. The captain went to the ladies who, as we now learned for the first time, were separated from us merely by a slender wooden partition, and asked them where he should take them. 'To the island of Murano,' was the reply, and the name of the house was mentioned. 'The island of Murano!' cried the Prince, and a shudder of premonition seemed to sweep through his soul. Before I could answer him, Biondello rushed in. 'Do you know in whose company we are travelling?' – The Prince sprang to his feet. – 'She is here! She herself!' continued Biondello. 'I have just spoken to her companion.'

The Prince hurried out. The room was too narrow for him – the whole world would have been too narrow in this instant. A thousand emotions stormed within him, his knees were trembling, his face was alternately flushed and pale. I too was trembling with shared expectancy. I cannot find words to describe our feelings to you.

The boat moored in Murano. The Prince leapt to shore. She came. I could read in the Prince's face that it was her. The sight of her left me with no doubt. A more beautiful shape have I never seen; all the Prince's descriptions had fallen short of the reality. A glowing blush suffused across her face as she caught sight of the Prince. She must have heard our entire conversation, and could not be in any doubt that she had been the subject of it. With a meaningful glance she looked at her companion, as if to say, 'That's him!' – and she shyly lowered her eyes. A narrow plank was laid from the ship to the shore, across which she had to walk. She seemed nervous about setting foot on it – but less, it seemed to me, because she was frightened she might slip than because she could not do it without someone's help, and the Prince was already stretching out his arm to assist her. Need triumphed over this hesitation. She accepted his hand and was soon on the shore. The vehement emotions sweeping through the Prince made him impolite; he quite forgot the other lady who was waiting for him to perform the same service – what would he *not* have forgotten at this moment? I finally offered her my arm, and this meant I lost the prologue of the conversation that had started up between my master and the lady.

He continued to hold her hand in his – distractedly, I think, and without himself being aware of it.

'This is not the first time, Signora, that – that – ' He could not say it.

'I ought to remember it,' she said faintly.

'In the ** Church –' said he.

'It was in the ** Church –' said she.

'And could I ever have imagined – being so near to you today –'

Here she gently took her hand out of his. – He was visibly bewildered. Biondello, who had meanwhile been talking to the servant, came to the rescue.

'Signore,' he began, 'the ladies have ordered sedan-chairs to come; but we have arrived back earlier than they had anticipated. There is a garden nearby, which you can go into for as long as you wish to avoid the crowds.'

The suggestion was accepted, and you can easily imagine with what alacrity on the part of the Prince. We stayed in the garden until it was evening. Z** and I succeeded in keeping the matron busy so that the Prince could converse undisturbed with the young lady. That he managed to make the best of these moments you can deduce from the fact that he was granted permission to go and visit her. Even now, as I write to you, he is there with her. When he returns, I will find out more.

Yesterday, when we came home, we also found the expected bills of exchange from our Court, but accompanied by a letter that made my master flare up in anger. He is being recalled, and in such a tone as he is quite unused to. He immediately replied in kind, and intends to stay put. The bills of exchange are just sufficient to pay the interest on the capital he owes. We impatiently await an answer from his sister.

Baron von F** to Count von O**
Letter Ten   SEPTEMBER

The Prince has fallen out with his Court, and all our resources from that quarter have been cut off.

The six weeks after which my master was due to pay the Marchese elapsed a few days ago, and there were still no bills of exchange either from his cousin, whom he had requested once again and most urgently for an advance, or from his sister. You will easily imagine that Civitella did not send a reminder, but the Prince had remembered all the more faithfully. Yesterday at noon an answer came from the authorities at Court.

We had shortly before signed a new agreement to remain in our hotel, and the Prince had publicly declared his intention to stay on longer. Without a word, my master gave me the letter. His eyes were sparkling, I could already read the contents on his brow.

Could you imagine it, my dear O**? In **, they are informed of all my master's doings here, and slanderous tongues have spun a repulsive web of lies out of them. They have heard with disapproval, it appears, among other things, that the Prince has for some time been starting to belie his previous character and adopt a behaviour that was quite the opposite of his hitherto exemplary outlook on life. It is known – they say – that he is indulging himself in the most dissipated way with women and gambling, is falling into debt, lending his ear to visionaries and necromancers, is involved in dubious relations with Catholic prelates, and is running a royal household that outstrips his rank as well as his income. It is even claimed that he is about to crown this exceedingly offensive conduct by apostasy to the Roman Catholic Church. So he can clear himself of this last charge, he is required to return without delay. A banker in Venice to whom he is to disclose the state of his debts has been given funds to satisfy his creditors *immediately after his departure*; for in these circumstances it is not thought a good idea to hand the money over to him.

What accusations, and made in such a tone! I took the letter, read it through once more, and wanted to find in it something that could soften its impact; I found nothing; it was quite incomprehensible to me.

Z** now reminded me of the secret enquiries that had been made of Biondello. The time, the content, all the circumstances agreed. We had falsely ascribed it all to the Armenian. Now it was clear whom it stemmed from. Apostasy! – But in whose interest can it be to slander my master in such a repellent and unimaginative way? I fear it is a trick of the Prince of **d**, who wants to push through his plan of forcing our Prince out of Venice.

The Prince fell silent again, his eyes staring ahead of him. His silence frightened me. I threw myself to his feet. 'For God's sake, my lord,' I exclaimed, 'do not decide on anything violent. You must and will have full satisfaction. Let *me* deal with this business. Send me as your envoy. It is beneath your dignity to have to answer such charges; but allow *me* to do it. The slanderer must be named and **'s eyes opened.'

Civitella found us in this state, and enquired in amazement what had caused our consternation. Z** and I were silent. But the Prince, who has long been accustomed to making no distinction between him and us and was still in too great a turmoil to listen to sensible advice right now, ordered us to share the contents of the letter with him. I hesitated, but the Prince tore it from my hand and himself handed it to the Marchese.

'I am in debt to you, Marchese,' the Prince began, when the latter had read through the letter with astonishment, 'but don't let that cause you any disquiet. Just grant me another twenty days' respite, and you will be satisfied.'

'My lord,' cried Civitella with considerable emotion, 'do I deserve this?'

'You did not want to send me a reminder; I acknowledge your delicacy and thank you for it. In twenty days, as I said, you will be fully satisfied.'

'How can this be?' asked Civitella, in the greatest consternation. 'What's the meaning of it all? I don't understand.'

We told him what we knew. He was beside himself. The Prince must, he said, insist on satisfaction from the Court; the insult was monstrous. Meanwhile he implored him to make use of all the wealth and credit at his disposal, without restriction.

The Marchese had left us and the Prince had still not uttered a word. He was pacing up and down the room; there was something extraordinary going on inside him. Finally he came to a halt and murmured between his teeth: ' "Congratulate yourself," he said. – "He died at nine o'clock." '

We gazed at him in shocked horror.

' "Congratulate yourself," ' he continued; 'congratulate myself – that's what I must do. – Isn't that what he said? What did he mean?'

'What makes you say that?' I cried. 'What does that have to do with anything?'

'I have never understood what the man was saying. Now I understand. – Oh, it is unbearably hard to have a master over oneself!'

'My dearest Prince!'

'That he can make us feel like this! – Ha! It must be sweet for him!'

He again stopped. His expression frightened me. I had never seen him look like that.

'The most wretched man among the common people,' he resumed, 'or the heir to the throne! It's all one and the same. There is only *one* difference between men – obeying or commanding!'

He looked at the letter again.

'You know the man,' he continued, 'who has dared to write this to me. Would you have greeted him on the street if fate had not made him your master? By God! There's something great in a crown!'

He carried on in this strain, and words fell from his lips that I cannot commit to a letter. But on this occasion the Prince revealed a circumstance to me that caused me no little amazement and fear, and that may have the most dangerous consequences. We had been hitherto completely mistaken about the family relations within the ** Court.

The Prince replied to the letter on the spot, however much I tried to dissuade him, and the way he did so means that no further amicable settlement can be hoped for.

You will now also be eager, dearest O**, to learn something definite about the Greek lady, but this is precisely a matter on which I can still give you no satisfactory details. Nothing can be got out of the Prince, as he is in on the secret and, I imagine, has had to promise to keep it. But that she is *not* the Greek we thought she was is now clear. She is a German, and of the noblest origin. A certain rumour that I managed to pick up says she has a mother of the highest rank, and claims that she is the fruit of an unhappy love affair, which has been the topic of much gossip in Europe. Secretly persecuted by a powerful figure, she has, according to the rumour, been compelled to take refuge in Venice, and the same persecution is also the reason why she is in hiding, which made it impossible for the Prince to discover where she is staying. The reverence with which the Prince speaks of her, and the way he shows a certain particular consideration towards her, seem to strengthen this supposition.

He is bound to her by a fearful passion which grows each day. At first, visits were sparingly granted, but already in the second week the periods of separation were being shortened, and now no day goes by without the Prince going to her house. Entire evenings go by without us catching a glimpse of him; and even if he isn't in her company, *she* it is who alone preoccupies him. His entire personality seems transformed. He goes round as if lost in a dream, and nothing of all that used to interest him can rouse even his fleeting attention.

Where will this all lead, dearest friend? I tremble for the future. The breach with his Court has placed my master in a humiliating dependency on a single man, the Marchese Civitella. The latter is now master of our secrets, of our entire fate. Will he always think so nobly as he still shows himself to? Will his good reputation prove durable, and is it a good thing to give a man, even the most excellent man, so much importance and power?

A new letter to the Prince's sister has left. I hope to be able to give you news of its success in my next letter.

The Count von O** continues:

But this next letter never came. Three whole months went by before I received news from Venice – an interruption whose cause became only too apparent later. All my friend's letters to me had been held back and suppressed. You can judge my consternation when finally, in the December of this year, I received the following missive, which only a lucky chance (as Biondello, who was to deliver it, suddenly fell ill) brought into my hands:

You do not write. You do not reply – Come – oh come on the wings of friendship. We have lost hope. Read this decision. We have lost all hope.

The Marchese's wound is deemed to be fatal. The Cardinal is brooding on vengeance, and his assassins are seeking the Prince. My master – oh my unfortunate master! – Has it come to this? Undeserved, dreadful fate! We must hide from murderers and creditors, like criminals.

I am writing to you from the ** Monastery, where the Prince has found refuge. At this moment he is resting on a hard bed next to me and sleeping – ah, the sleep of the deadliest exhaustion, that will merely replenish his strength so he can awaken to feel his sufferings anew. The ten days that she was ill, he did not sleep a wink. I was present at the autopsy. Traces of poisoning were found. She is to be buried today.

Ah, dearest O**, my heart is broken. I have experienced a scene that will never fade from my memory. I stood in front of her deathbed. She died like a saint, and she used her last dying eloquence to lead her beloved along the path that she was following to heaven. – All our fortitude was shattered, the Prince alone preserved his composure, and even if he shared the sufferings of her death threefold with her, he nonetheless maintained enough strength of mind to deny the pious enthusiast her last request.

In this letter was the following resolution:

To the Prince of ** from his sister:

The Church outside of which there is no salvation, that has made such a brilliant conquest in the Prince of **, will also ensure that he is not short of the means of persisting in the way of life to which she owes that conquest. I have tears and prayers for a man who has gone astray, but no more favours for an unworthy man.

– Henriette **

I immediately took a mail-coach, travelled night and day, and in the third week I was in Venice. My urgent haste came too late to be of any use. I had come to bring consolation and help to an unhappy man; I found a happy one who no longer needed my feeble assistance. F** was ill in bed when I arrived, and I could not speak to him; the following note he had written was given to me: 'Return, dearest O**, whence you came. The Prince does not need you any more, nor me. His debts have been paid, the Cardinal reconciled, the Marchese has quite recovered. Do you remember the Armenian, who managed to perplex us so badly last year? In *his* arms you will find the Prince who five days ago – heard his first mass.'

I tried to force my way through to the Prince all the same, but was turned away. At the bedside of my friend I finally heard the incredible story.

1. At this time there was a black-robed Armenian sect with a monastery in Venice (San Lazzaro). This sect recognised the authority of the Pope, and the 'Armenian' in Schiller's story doubtless forms part of the 'Catholic plot' subtext.

2. Schiller based his impostor figure on Cagliostro, whose dabblings in the occult and associated confidence tricks also had political repercussions and, in the Affair of the Diamond Necklace of 1785, may have helped to bring the French monarchy into even greater pre-Revolutionary disrepute than it already was. Cagliostro also passed himself off as a Prussian or Spanish officer.

3. This was Clement XIV (1769–74) who dissolved the Jesuit order in 1772; one version has it that they took their revenge by poisoning him.

4. The white apron in this instance would have been similar to those worn by Freemasons (and Cagliostro).

5. Apollonius of Tyana (*fl.* first century AD) was a Pythagorean magician from the time of Nero.

6. *Comte de Gabalis*, by Abbé de Montfauconde de Villars, is a collection of discourses, first published in Paris in 1670, on the subject of the 'Secret Sciences'.

7. It has been suggested that this 'unknown musical instrument' was in fact a glass harmonica, whose ethereal and haunting sounds made it popular in the late eighteenth century.

8. From Tacitus' *Germania*: 'what it is that only those who are about to die can see'.

9. Faro was a popular eighteenth-century card-game (named after the 'Pharaohs' depicted on the cards).

Johann Christoph Friedrich von Schiller was born in 1759, the son of an army captain. He attended the Duke of Württemberg's military academy where he was forced to embark upon a career in medicine. After his graduation in 1780, he was given a position as an army surgeon, but he abhorred the military life, and instead sought refuge in writing. *Die Räuber* (*The Robbers*), a fervent attack on political tyranny, appeared in 1781, and it was this dramatic work in particular that led to his position as the leading figure of the *Sturm und Drang* (Storm and Stress) movement of German literature. Performed to great public acclaim in 1782, *Die Räuber* however greatly displeased the Duke who immediately forbade Schiller to continue writing.

Fleeing from his post, Schiller took up a position with the Mannheim Theatre, working as a dramatist. *Don Carlos*, another successful piece, followed soon after, and was performed in a revised version in 1787. Schiller then turned his hand to history, producing such works as *The Revolt of the Netherlands* and *A History of the Thirty Years War*. His ensuing success led to a professorship at the University of Jena (now the Friedrich Schiller University) in 1789.

The following year he married the writer Charlotte von Lengefeld, but his poor health prevented him from taking up any further academic positions. With Charlotte he settled in Weimar, and in 1794 developed a strong friendship with Goethe. The latter proved a strong influence on Schiller's writing, persuading him to return to dramatic works. The plays that followed, including *The Piccolomini* (1799), *Mary Stuart* (1800) and *William Tell* (1804), are some of the finest examples of Schiller's craft, exemplifying his favoured theme of the problem of freedom and responsibility. In 1805 Schiller contracted tuberculosis and he died on 9 May at the age of forty-six.

Andrew Brown studied at the University of Cambridge, where he taught French for many years. He now works as a teacher and translator. He is the author of *Roland Barthes: the Figures of Writing* (OUP, 1993) and his translations include Zola's *For a Night of Love*, Gautier's *The Jinx*, and Gide's *Theseus*, all published by Hesperus Press.

HESPERUS PRESS – 100 PAGES

Hesperus Press, as suggested by the Latin motto, is committed to bringing near what is far – far both in space and time. Works written by the greatest authors, and unjustly neglected or simply little known in the English-speaking world, are made accessible through new translations and a completely fresh editorial approach. Through these short classic works, each little more than 100 pages in length, the reader will be introduced to the greatest writers from all times and all cultures.

For more information on Hesperus Press, please visit our website:
www.hesperuspress.com

ET REMOTISSIMA PROPE

SELECTED TITLES FROM HESPERUS PRESS